DARCY

HARRISON AMBUSH BOOK 4

KATHI S. BARTON

World Castle Publishing, LLC
Pensacola, Florida
Copyright © Kathi S. Barton 2016
Paperback ISBN: 9781629895956
eBook ISBN: 9781629895963
First Edition World Castle Publishing, LLC, November 28, 2016
http://www.worldcastlepublishing.com
Licensing Notes
Cover: Karen Fuller
Editor: Maxine Bringenberg

PROLOGUE

"Here, let me show you. You have to remember, Brooke, that you weigh a tad more than that little bit of mud. Just lay your weight over it like I showed you, and center your start." She did that, bending her body nearly in half to do it. However, she was too short and couldn't get the clay to center correctly no matter what she tried. Standing up and leaning over the wheel again, she got it to do just what she wanted. But she knew that doing it this way was going to hurt her back. Brooke looked at her grandda and asked him for some help.

"Okay, so you have to stand. We can work around that." He nodded as he took measurements of her and the height of the wheel. "Heard tell that some potters stand when they throw. Me? Can't do it no matter how old I get. But you, I think you can make it work for you, being that you're young starting it this way."

It took them two weeks to get the wheel at the right height for her. Every little adjustment was written on the wall beside the kilns and then dated. They were going to get it perfect for her, and she had no doubt that she'd be throwing pots right alongside her grandda before too much longer.

After a month she was pulling up the long line of clay almost as well as Grandda. He was letting her experiment with forms and some of the tools he'd made on his own too. Brooke felt like a real potter when he treated her this way…like she was his partner, not just his great granddaughter.

Some of his tools were as old as her, others as old as her mom would have been had she not died. When Brooke asked him about other designs that she wanted to make, he showed her that as well. Not only how to make the small wooden tools that were as standard in a pottery shed as the clay would be, but how to use the things that were right outside their door.

When she threw her first large piece, one that she was as proud of as anything she'd ever done, he stood back and looked at it. It wasn't finished, not by a long shot, as it was still raw, the clay only just beginning to turn leather hard. When he walked around it for the fourth time, not saying anything but really looking at it, Brooke looked too. She could see every line of it, every little finger mark, and where she had paused with the wet sponge in the process. Pausing in front of it, his hand on his cheek, she knew that Grandda was going to tell her she could do much better, which she could, and that someday she might be half as good as him.

"What's your plan? I mean, when you had that raw ball in your hand, what did it say to you?" Grandda had told her that each piece spoke to him. Even before he knew what it was going to be, the clay did. Brooke looked at the forms she'd thrown and tried to think how to tell him what she thought it said. "Come on now, you know that of all people, I'll understand what it said."

"I'm to keep it like it is, raw for now, at least until it's firm enough for me to work with. Then I'm to put some of the stones in it that I found in the mountain." He nodded, still not looking at her but at the piece. "When I fire it, the clay said that the colors will be like none other…that once we take it from the fire it'll show a brilliance that the earth has never seen."

Grandda walked around the piece once more. It was going to be tall, about five feet with all the pieces stacked atop one another. The batts, the board that she'd used to throw it on, was still attached until it was dry enough to remove.

She'd had to throw three pieces to get it the way she had seen it in her head, each of them a little different, a little wider or taller, but they would stack atop one another to get the height she knew it had to be. And it wasn't a clean fit…the clay hadn't allowed her to be perfect about her technique. Now, it was in its last stages of drying enough to work with, to put the final art on before it had to be put in a kiln to fire the first time. Brooke could see what stone to use as well as where it was to be put in the clay before the final firing, the one that would bring it to life.

"When you're finished, I want to help you with it." She nodded, hoping that he'd say that. "Not the finishing touches, but with the firing. It will take a delicate firing, slow to burn and hot. You'll need to stay with me when we do this; the fire cannot ever cool too much or get too high. The kiln, it will need to be watched over, like the pieces that we fill it with. You willing to do that? To come and be a part of its next journey?"

"Yes. I want to do this." He nodded and looked at the piece again before turning to her. "You think it will be a nice piece? Not show quality like yours, but nice?"

"Never say that it will not be perfect before you even see it. The clay, it has a heart, same as you. Otherwise why would we bother?" She nodded, not sure what he meant. "It will be what it wants to be, using you as its canvas, not the other way around. All right?"

She nodded. Yes, she was the way for the clay to speak, not her to speak to it.

Over the next three days she gathered her stones, laying them out in the order that she could see in her head. She'd tried to plan them out on her own, matching the colors in groups, the size of them going from smaller to larger. But her muse, her clay, wouldn't let her finish when she tried to change the design to suit herself. The piece, it seemed, knew just the way it was to be.

The day before the firing, a full month after Grandda had said he wanted to help her, he and Brooke had started the fires in the lower part of the kiln. Lucky for her there were enough pieces to fill the cave kiln. Otherwise she might have had to wait for several more months to see her finished piece.

Her grandda had built the kiln in the forties when there wasn't one big enough to fire the pieces that he wanted to glaze. He designed his own anagama kiln, built right into the mountain and fed at the bottom in a continuous feeding of wood, when no builder would help him. He and several other potters, all but him now out of business, had spent the better part of a year digging out the cave and making a fire pit large enough to heat it to the right temperatures. The fuel, mostly trees felled on the property where the kiln was built, was perfect for the firings. Each different type of wood would add a chemical product to the firing that could never be duplicated. It was what made this type of firing so amazing.

They would get ash from the wood, and salts that mixed with the chemicals of the glazes would give colors that might never be seen in an electric or gas fired kiln. Even a raku firing — one where the piece was heated to a certain temperature then taken out, almost molten, to be dropped in different elements such as newspapers or straws — couldn't compare to a wood firing.

It took three days for the anagama kiln to cool enough to

open; the same number of days it had taken for it to get to temperature. She went from wishing the process would hurry to just wishing that it had never been fired. Brooke was afraid of what they might find inside.

There were hundreds of pieces in the large kiln that had been brought in by local potters, schools, as well as people just starting out in this sort of medium. Some of them had brought their work to them months ago, others just that morning. Things had been busy getting the kiln loaded. Grandda's rule was, you want it fired, then you help with the firing. Which meant chopping wood, loading the pottery, staying up when it was your turn to stoke the fire, as well as help out with the food. There was always plenty of that latter to go around too.

Pieces would be put in, sitting on the steps up the high hill, stacked on large shelves, or even buried in the dirt so that the effect would, hopefully, be amazing. The heat would reach each piece, while the fumes, some of them noxious, would be vented out of the top, nearly at the peak of their mountain.

Each piece had been marked because sometimes months would go by and they'd have to remind the person that their pieces were ready to be fired. Brooke had met a great many famous men and women when they'd come to their farm to party with their grandda during a long firing, and had remained friends with them long after.

Brooke knew that it wasn't going to be a quick firing, as he'd told her slow and delicate was needed. And when they were satisfied that they'd done all they could for the pieces, not just hers but all pieces in the kiln, they let the flames slow to a low burn for another day, then let it die all together. All they could do now was wait.

Upon opening the great door, there were shattered pieces just inside the doorway. Broken shards of pottery, some of it melded to another piece of work and ruining both pieces of art. Walls of pottery were still too hot to touch, while others had cooled enough to be removed with heavy asbestos gloves. Brooke tried to avoid the area where her pieces were sitting. Her piece, her first, was in the middle, still some feet from where they'd entered.

"You know, child, that not all of my pieces make it out of here. That is the worst kind of torture for an artist, to find that something happened in the firing and it's all for naught." She told him that she understood that, but she'd still be disappointed. "As you should be. It's a fine piece you put together. I hope we can display it in the store in town."

It would be an honor to have her work displayed in the store, Brooke knew this. But no one, except a select few, would ever know that it was hers. It was the way her grandda had lived his artistic life, and the same way she would live hers, she'd decided. Being famous, she'd always believed, had gotten her mom nowhere but dead, and that was enough limelight for her.

She saw the first of the three pieces sitting just where she'd put it. Walking slowly to it, Brooke held her breath until she saw the second one. It too seemed to be all right; nothing had been broken around it, and hers had survived and not exploded onto someone else's. Then she stood over the third.

"Brooke?" Grandda stood beside her as they looked at the pieces. They were all complete, with nothing touching them. Her first piece had fired well. "We can't take it out just yet, a couple more hours. We have to be careful that it doesn't get a cool breeze, either."

Stacking the pieces up in the store had been more than she could have hoped for. The stones had lent a natural element to it that she hadn't seen in her visions of it done. Some of them had melted just a little, leaving the holes that she'd set them in with a beautiful watery dripped look. The glazes that she'd sprayed on it before putting it in the kiln had given the piece a matte look in some places, and a bright shiny glaze in others. The ash from the wood along with the salt from the mountain had also changed many of the colors to be entirely different than the clay had told her about. Matching the stones and other elements on it had given it a very earthy look. Brooke was so proud of it that she'd taken several pictures and had them printed and framed.

The piece stood in the front of the store for two weeks. People had come in asking how they'd found such a wonderful Rickson piece. She'd had so much pride in those comments that she'd taken to putting a penny in a jar each time she heard it. It wouldn't ever be much, but it was something akin to having them know it was her.

The price on it, only a token one really, tripled what she wanted for it, had she really wanted to let it go. Brooke had no plans to sell it, so when a man had come from some large pottery shop and paid her price, she was both excited and sad at the same time. But the money had gone to getting more supplies for their shop, and she'd sold her first piece. It wouldn't always be that way, she knew this, but now she had a goal, a bigger one than before the sale. To make enough money to pay for her own supplies, as well as a part of the monthly bills on the shop.

Brooke knew she was well on her way to becoming someone her grandda could be proud of. But she also knew that no matter what she did or didn't do, her grandda would love her with all his heart.

CHAPTER 1

Mac tugged at his tie. It wasn't uncomfortable, it was just that he wasn't used to wearing one anymore. He wore a suit coat and pants to work when he had to, but lately they'd all been wearing just polos. When he and Darcy were in the front of the line to go inside the large building, a young woman approached them after their tickets were taken.

"Hello, Mr. Harrison?" He nodded. "My name is Olivia. I'm to understand that you might have a piece of pottery that you want verified?" She showed him her identification, saying that she worked for Rickson Pottery.

"Verified? I guess." Mac handed her the vase after unwrapping it. "When will I get to talk to the person who can tell me when it was made?"

"Let's not get ahead of ourselves here. We have to make sure that this isn't a forgery. You'd be surprised how many people bring in pieces that they made themselves to try and pass off." He didn't care for her tone, nor the implication that he was trying to scam someone. "I'll find you when we get finished with this."

"Well that was rude, don't you think?" Mac agreed with Darcy. "You think they truly get a lot of forged pottery in this market? I can understand paintings and glass things, I guess. But pottery?"

13

"Yeah, I do. And you're right, she might have been a good deal nicer about it. As well as being a little less accusatory toward us. But I know some of the pieces can be really expensive. The piece I have was appraised at about two grand a couple of years ago." Darcy and he started walking around the huge gallery. "I still can't believe that Nikki was able to get us in here. This is the best early Christmas I've had in a while."

"Yeah, it's too bad that Andi couldn't come. But I'm also glad that she didn't. Thanks again for bringing me along with you. This is great." They paused in front of a piece that was about six feet tall. "Christ, can you imagine trying to throw something like that?"

"It says here that it was thrown in pieces, then stacked after each piece was glazed and fired. The art on it was done prior to the firing process, and then restacked once the glaze firing was complete. It was fired in an anagama kiln, a handmade kiln that is usually built in the side of a mountain. It says that the artist is never sure if the art will line up perfectly until it's complete." Mac looked at the gorgeous scene of a mountain side covered in trees and a waterfall tumbling down from it. He thought he could almost feel the water spraying in his face. "This took the potter nine days to finish after the forms were thrown, adding on each piece of the water and trees carefully so that the clay wasn't stressed and didn't fall in on itself as it was worked."

"Wow, that's gorgeous. I can see that sitting in your living room right in front of that big window. It matches that room perfectly." Darcy turned it over and saw the price. "It has a sold ticket on it. I thought this was just an exhibit of the work. And I guess you were right about the prices. This one is nearly seventy grand."

"This is an exhibit for the most part, but once the flyers go out and people see the work, there are always a few that call and make an offer. I'm not entirely sure why the artist agreed to leave it on the floor even after it was paid for. This piece was sold before it was even in the house, or the gallery." They both turned to look at Olivia when she spoke. "Mr. Harrison, your piece is authentic, so would you please follow me?"

Darcy declined to come along, saying that he wanted to look around some more. When Mac and Olivia were at a door in the back of the gallery, she turned to him and asked him for his cell phone or any other recording devices. Actually, it was more of a demand, but he took a step back from her.

"My phone? I don't think so. I don't know you, and I have a pregnant wife at home that might need me." The door opened and a man stood there looking at the woman for several seconds before looking at him. He didn't speak, but did wave him inside. Without a glance at Olivia, he went inside to have the door closed after him and the other man. "She is not a nice person."

"No, she's not. And I'm sorry for that. Her mom was fired this morning, and Olivia isn't taking it any better than Mary did." Mac turned to where the voice came from and a light flared on. He nearly said something very rude himself when he got a look at the woman standing there. Christ, she was perfection. "My name is Brooke, this is my brother, Brody. I'd like to talk to you about your piece. Can you tell me how you acquired it?"

"I didn't steal it if that's what you're asking me." She laughed and said that she hadn't thought he had. "I'm sorry. I'm not normally this rude to strangers. That woman, she put me a little on edge with her questions and comments. I bought it about fifteen years ago at an estate sale. The man who had it in his collection had gotten it in the mountains about thirty years ago or so. I'm sorry, the Smokey Mountains. His family hated to part with it, I was told, but since no one could agree on who got it, they had to sell by law. Really sucks for them, but I was able to pick it up."

"That sounds about right. It's old...more than likely, as they told you, from about the thirties or forties. It's a raku piece, fired in an outside kiln and then dropped in what I think was straw when it was still fairly hot. It was Mr. Rickson's favorite medium" He knew that. Mac told her how the family had given him the story about the piece when he'd gotten it. Brody left them then, saying that he needed air. When she didn't say anything, neither did he. Brody had seemed...well, he seemed antsy about being in the room with them.

"Did you know that it's cracked? Just a ping crack, it's called. Sometimes with high fire clay there are what we call stress fractures. It could be just the clay not settling right, or more than likely in this case, the clay cooled down too quickly. With a raku firing, you would lose about ten percent of your pieces to that very thing."

She held it up to a light, then showed him how the piece, when cracked, would sound differently when it was bumped gently against something. He sat down when she did.

"Will it break completely if I don't let anything happen to it?" She said it was hard to tell, but it more than likely would. Clay was a very unpredictable thing. "I would guess that painting and other forms of art are much more stable."

"They are. Even with the crack, it's still worth a great deal. Fifty grand...more if it wasn't cracked. If you wish to sell it, I'd gladly buy it from you." He looked around the room, then at his piece. Fifty grand? Christ. "As I said, it's a very old piece."

He didn't want to sell it. He and Andi were having a room addition put on their house just for his collection, and this

16

piece was the center of it all. Mac loved pottery. It mattered little to him if it was from someone famous or not, he just liked it. But this piece, a Rickson, was the most beautiful of all his collection, he thought.

Mac looked at Brooke. She was beautiful, like model beautiful, with long dark, almost blue black hair that hung at her back in a thick braid. Her skin was what his dad might have called porcelain, perfect against the darkness of her hair. High cheekbones and a small button nose adorned her face, but it was her eyes that captured one's attention. Purple, a deep amethyst color that seemed to change just a little with the tilt of her head. Mac remembered the man and then his name.

"You said that Brody was your brother." She nodded but he could see her getting tense. "Olivia wanted my phone, so I couldn't take any pictures. Not of the things in here, but of you. Just you, I think. I wonder why she'd do that? Or for that matter, why you'd have her do it? And you did, didn't you?"

"Perhaps I just didn't want you to record what I said about your pottery. Or maybe I didn't want you posting pictures of me without my permission. It's all very simple, I think." Mac shook his head. "I will buy the piece from you, Mr. Harrison, but no more than what it's worth."

"I'm sorry, but it's not for sale. And I think I'm right about this and you. Your name, it starts with a B. So does...." Mack looked around the room, then at her. "Brooke Rickson. You're BG Rickson. You're the expert because he's your...not your father; he had to be a good deal too old for that. So he was your grandfather, I think."

"Great grandfather. How did you know about me? Or Brody? We.... Are you trying to blackmail me too? If so, you aren't going to get anything either. Or did Uncle Blake send you?" She stood up and so did he. "You can tell him what I did

KATHI S. BARTON

before I left home, as well as the million other times that he has hurt me. I'm not going to give him anything. Grandda left it to me, not him, for a reason."

"I'm not trying to blackmail you, nor do I want to harm you in any way. And I don't know who this Blake person is other than what I read about him, but if you need help with him, I can find it for you." She asked him who had told him while tears fell down her cheeks. It broke his heart to know that he'd upset her this way. "My sister-in-law is a cop. She did some digging when my wife told her about my love of Rickson. Brooke, you're the Running Water Pottery too, aren't you? Rickson, he named it for you."

She moved around the room, touching the pieces in the room with such a gentle hand that it was hard to believe that it was stoneware and not something like silk or glass. When she paused in front of his piece, she didn't turn to look at him while she spoke. She was still crying and he hated that so much.

"Grandda taught me all he knew when I was just a little girl. Not just about pottery, but about life and things in general. I suppose in a way he was sort of jaded about many things, people mostly. But he was all I had, so I tended to listen to him and take his words to heart. But the Running Water pottery is named for my mom, not me. She died a few days after my brother was born. We were living with him when.... Anyway, I lived with him my whole life after she died, Brody too. Benson...I guess you could say that he spent a great deal of his time with our uncle when he wasn't hiding from someone in the mountains. Or, like most of the time, he would bum someone's couch and stay there until they caught him stealing from them." She ran her finger down the piece, almost like a caress. "Great Grandda died almost a month ago. Just before he did, he begged me to come to this exhibit to show off both

18

of our work, mostly his, one more time. Then he told me that I'd be safe, that no one would ever connect the dots to me."

"Nikki, my sister-in-law, is very good. She didn't know your name, only that you were B to his D. What does the G stand for?" She told him as she sat back in her seat. "Brooke Grace Rickson, it's wonderful to meet you."

She was upset, he knew this. It was written all over her face and in every line of her body. He wanted to tell her that he'd not share her secret, and that he'd take it to the grave, but he had a feeling that she wouldn't believe him, that she'd been told that line before. Mac was ready to tell her, explain to her that she could trust him, when Darcy touched his head, full of panic.

I need you out here, now. Mac stood up and so did Brooke. *Christ, I'm going to jail, I just fucking know it. Call an ambulance too.*

"Stay here. There's a problem out front." He should have known that she'd follow him. The women in his family, including his wife, would have mopped the floor up with him had he said anything like that to them. "All right, but please call an ambulance. I guess we need one."

He was out the door before she'd picked up the phone. Mac was told to come to the room on the right of where he'd been taken, but to tread carefully. As he made his way to the room, Mac encountered three wolves, all of them men, and it looked as if they were standing guard at the door. It wasn't until one of them sniffed the air around him that he was allowed in.

As soon as he was in the room with who he thought was alpha to the wolves, Mac saw his brother. The alpha, Morgan he said his name was, told him that he'd wanted to make sure that no one knew what was going on so as not to cause a scene. Mac thanked him. He had a feeling that this man knew Brooke

19

and her desire to keep her identity secret.

Mac saw the vase and the stand it had been sitting on broken on the floor, its blue pieces shattered all over the place. The young man, Brody, was against the wall, unconscious but otherwise all right, his heart beating at a normal pace. That was when he saw his brother on top of a stranger.

Darcy had played football in both high school and college, so to see him atop a man, holding him down with his arm around his neck and his knee in his back, didn't make him as nervous as the gun lying no more than four feet from them. There was a long baton there as well, something he'd seen both Nikki and Storm use when they were taking down a jackass. Crouching down, he asked Darcy if he was all right.

"Yeah, I'm just fine and dandy. This shit, however, I don't think he's doing so well." Darcy nodded to the other man. "He hit him. Just came in the door and knocked the kid on his ass like he was nothing at all."

Brooke went to her brother just as he was coming around, Mac noticed. When Brody let her look at him, even from where he was Mac could tell that his arm was broken. Mac asked the man under Darcy who he was.

"Benson Rickson. Where the fuck is my sister?" Mac was glad that he'd stood between Brooke and the man. He had no idea why, but he figured he'd try to knock Darcy off and hurt both of them. "She owes me some money and I want it now, not when she gets back to her house. Get her for me. And get this piece of fucking shit off me too."

Darcy laughed. "I don't think you understand the way this works. Usually, when I have a man in a headlock, he asks nicely for things. You know, like 'Would you please let me go so that I can breathe?' Or maybe, 'Can you get off my back? You're hurting me and I'd really appreciate it if you'd not hurt me more.' Perhaps, and this is what I'm thinking, I'm not doing this right." Benson screamed when Darcy moved, and Mac laughed. "There you go. Just what I wanted, you to understand that I'm the one in charge, not you. Now what were you saying about your sister?"

Before either of them could speak, Brooke came to where they were and kicked Benson in the head. It wasn't as bad as the man made it sound, but he did try unsuccessfully to get out from under Darcy to get her.

"Benson, you're not supposed to be here. I told you, several times, that I have a restraining order against you and you're to keep one mile away from me. Do you know how much that is? I think you were given a lesson on that not long ago by our police department when you tried to get into my home. And it is my home, Benson...I know you've had that explained to you as well." Mac looked up at Brooke when she said his name. "Can you please ask him not to let Benson go until the police get here? I don't know what he'll do if he's free."

"Yes, ma'am, I can hold him. That other man, is he all right?" She told Darcy that he was hurting, but was going to be fine once his arm was taken care of. "I just bet he is. This fool came in here screaming about his sister...well, I won't repeat what he said. But when he didn't get any satisfaction in that, he pulled out that baton and started swinging it. I'm sorry about that piece. I didn't see what he was doing until it was already down."

"It wasn't one of the more priceless pieces, thankfully. But still vandalism. I guess this is why we have insurance on these things, in the event things like this happen." She kicked Benson again. "I'm sure you know this is not going to get you anything more than it would have before, don't you? Christ, you piss me off so much."

21

Mac stood up when the police arrived. Benson was still screaming at his sister, but he no longer called her names. The first time he did that when Darcy was holding him, he'd held him tightly enough that he blacked out. When he came to, Darcy explained to the man how he could kill him and make it look like an accident if he didn't stop using that sort of language around a lady. Apparently, he believed him.

Mac stood back while Benson was dealt with. Brody was taken by ambulance to the local hospital, and Brooke went with him on the promise that she'd meet the police there. By the time Darcy was finished telling them several times what had happened, the gallery had emptied out and Mac and Darcy were left alone with the staff and wolf pack. The wolf and his small pack had done just as they had promised. No one that had been there, other than them, had any idea what had happened. Or to who.

"Now what?" Darcy said he didn't know, but was sort of hungry. "Yeah, I could eat too. But do you think we can swing by the hospital? Just to make sure that Brooke is all right?"

Driving to the hospital, he told his brother what he and Brooke had talked about. Darcy, like him, was impressed that she'd been able to keep herself a secret all this time, and wondered what the hell was up with the brother. Mac shrugged as they pulled in the parking lot. Who knew the mind of some people? Greed, he figured, would make most people do a lot of strange things.

The hospital was busy. It was Friday night so he supposed that was usual. But when he was ready to just call it a night, not having any idea how to go about seeing her, Morgan stepped up to his car.

"You are the men who helped Running Water. I'm glad that you have come here." Mac nodded and felt his cat running

22

along his skin. "I wish to thank you. She does not know the evilness that her brother can do to her. Her heart hurts because he thinks so little of her and her grandfather. But her uncle, Blake, will not stop until he gets what he thinks he deserves."

"I'm thinking that she might have an idea about his evilness, but not how to handle him. Are you her mate?" Morgan said he wasn't and left it at that. "We just came by to make sure she was all right. I was talking to Brooke about something when he attacked their brother. I can leave if you think she's too stressed right now."

"No, I think it will mean a great deal to her to see you again. And I think she wishes to thank you both as well. Running Water, she does not trust well, nor does she venture far from home if she can avoid it. She did this to honor a promise to a great man, but I do not think even he could have foreseen such a thing to happen." Mac told him what Brooke had said about her great grandfather. "Then she trusts you. For that alone, I will as well. But I will be close at hand."

Not really a threat. It might have been if Mac had any intentions of hurting Brooke, but he didn't. So Mac took the man's words to mean just that. He'd be close should something else happen. Mac had no idea why, but he thought this was just the tip of the iceberg.

~~~

Darcy wanted to shift and hurt someone. It wasn't that he didn't like the wolf—he seemed like an all right guy—but he could tell that the man was on edge, and that made his cat a little pissy with him. His cat had been out for blood earlier, and now there was a wolf here telling him that the man he'd tangled with was evil.

When Morgan leaned back in the chair to wait, Darcy said he was going to take a short walk. Heading to the vending

23

machines to get something to tide him over, he saw the woman again, leaning against the wall sobbing. Careful not to startle her, he was nearly to her when her scent hit him square in the face. It took him a full minute to figure out what the hell it was.

His mate. Christ, the goddess standing there crying was his mate. Moving closer to her, his body and cat needing to give her comfort, Darcy tried to think what he was supposed to do now. Not upsetting her more was going to be first and foremost.

"Hello?" She turned and looked at him, and he felt his heart twist in his chest. "I'm Darcy Harrison…you met me and my brother Mac earlier. We came by to see if you were all right. Is there anything I can do?"

"Kill my brother?" He didn't say what he really wanted to, that he'd gladly do that for her, but she shook her head. "Benson is getting more violent all the time. He's mad that Grandda left everything to me and nothing to him. But there was no reason to hurt Brody. And to come into the gallery like he did…He could have hurt someone else, but he doesn't care about anything but himself. Nothing at all."

"I'm assuming that your grandfather had a good reason for not leaving him anything." He moved closer to her, careful not to touch her just yet no matter how much he really needed to. Darcy was a big man, and while she was tall, over six foot he'd bet, she was a small thing compared to him. "Would you like to go and get something to drink? Like a coffee or tea?"

"I don't drink coffee, and the tea here is shit." He laughed, he'd already figured that out. "Yes, Grandda had a good reason. While he was alive, Grandda had bailed him and my uncle out of every scrap there was, from robbing one of the local shops to hit and run accidents that they claimed weren't their fault. Nothing is ever their fault, I've come to realize;

24

everyone, according to them, is out to make them look bad. Christ, how stupid do they think people are? And then when he died and the will was read...." She paused and he waited for her to continue. When she only stared out the window that she'd been near, Darcy started talking.

"My brother and I came down here from Nashport, a little town not far from here. Nikki, my sister-in-law, was able to snag two tickets for Mac and his wife, Andi, to come here, but there was this shopping thing that my other sisters-in-law and my mom had planned to attend. So that's why I'm here." Darcy wanted to laugh...the fates had really done a number on him. "You were saying that your uncle and brother were into trouble."

"I have no idea why I'm telling you this." He did, but said nothing to her. "I'm usually so closed mouth about personal things. I talk to Morgan, but not to strangers like this. Morgan and his pack, they live on Granddda's...well, I guess they live on my land now."

"Perhaps you just trust me more because we've been there for you when things were down." She said nothing but continued to stare out the window. "Morgan, he's here too. Just so you know, he talked to my brother and me when we got here and told us to come in and wait. He said that he made sure that no one knew what was going on tonight, nor did he or his men let anyone come into the room to be nosy."

"He's a wolf, did you know that?" He said that he knew it. "I'm assuming, and I have no idea why, but you're not human either, are you? But not wolf. If you were then you would have said that."

"No, I'm not a wolf, but a tiger. My family are Bengals, pureblood." She nodded. "You never answered me...are you all right?"

"No, not really. I knew this was going to be a mistake. I just never realized how much it would cost me. But I'll be better when I get back to the mountain." He said nothing, but thought of all the things he had to close up in Ohio to be with her. Taking another step to her, he asked about Morgan. "He was a friend of my mom's. Well, Grandda's first, but he became my mother's protector too when Uncle Blake got it in his head to be a bastard. My dad, he died a while ago, just before she did actually. I never knew either of them. Morgan is the alpha of the pack on our...my land. I've known him all my life."

"Does Morgan have a large pack?" He had no idea why he was asking her this. Darcy didn't really care, but he was moving closer to her and didn't want to scare her. He figured she'd had enough frights for one night. "I've seen some pretty large packs up where I live. They roam my oldest brother's land all the time. I have five brothers. We're nearly an ambush all on our own."

"Ambush? I thought cats were called a streak?" He told her that he had no idea why they had chosen ambush over streak. "I guess it doesn't matter much, really. I mean, a group of bears is called a sloth or a sleuth. So who knows anymore?"

He laughed with her and reached out to touch his fingers to her cheek. It was as soft as he'd thought it would be, and she looked up at him. There was a little fear there, as well as confusion. Darcy could understand them both...he was feeling a little off himself.

"Running Water?" She turned her head and Darcy felt the breath he'd been holding slowly leave his body. He felt her nearness and her heat all the way to his toes. Darcy turned to Morgan when she did, and the wolf looked at him oddly, then nodded. "Your brother is asking after you. And I wish to tell you that Benson has called Blake as his only phone call. From what I am understanding, neither man has the bail money, so you should be prepared to be asked again for some of yours."

"The show is tomorrow night. He'll be there until then, right?" Morgan said that he would be if he had anything to do about it. Brooke turned to Darcy. "You saved me a great deal of grief tonight. I would be honored if you and your brother could come to the opening tomorrow night."

"Opening? I thought that was tonight." She explained that it was a pre-showing, that only special ticket holders were invited to it and could come to the opening should they want. "Well, how lucky have we been? Yes, Mac and I would love to come to the opening. Thank you."

CHAPTER 2

"I don't understand what you're telling me." Brooke was packing up her things. As soon as this was finished tonight she was going home. It would be a long drive, but she needed to be someplace safe for her peace of mind. And home was the only place where she felt that anymore. "You're saying that Darcy is something more to me than a really nice man? What is it he wants from me?"

"He wants everything that you are willing to give, I would guess. But what I am telling you is that he is your mate. You know as well as I do what that means, Running Water. You are his other half, his mate for life." Brooke said nothing. Whatever he was to her made no difference in what she was going to do with her own life. He would just have to deal with not having her, and she told Morgan that. "You know that it does not work that way. Once a male or female has found their mate, there will be no dealing, as you have called it. It is much too late for you to wish otherwise."

"I don't have to be anything to him. In fact, I'd just as soon he'd leave things the way they are." She thought about him touching her cheek and how it had made her feel. "He more than likely has no idea anyway. He would have told me last night had that been true."

"I think he is an honorable man and is taking things slowly.

Not because he wants to, but because he knows that you need for him to. When he touched you, Running Water, did you feel anything toward him?" She nodded, and wanted to tell him that she'd felt it all. Not just his touch, but that every part of her had seemed to come alive. "When you come together, it will be more."

"I don't think I want more. Just that much was pretty intense." She turned to look at Morgan and sat down. "I don't want anyone else in my life telling me what to do. Where to live and how to do that. I have things just the way I like them. If you don't count Benson and Blake, my life is pretty much perfect."

"They are going to be more trouble for you now. I have heard from the pack and Blake has been trying his best to get onto the property, without success. He will however, someday, and we will need to kill him." She knew that as well. "Your grandda, he would have done so already had he known half of what he has done to you."

"Grandda died thinking we were at peace. If given it to do over, I would have done the same. It gave him what he needed to stop trying to protect me so hard and just let go." Morgan nodded. "Besides, how was I to know that he left everything to me? I thought he'd at least take care of them. I can understand now why he didn't. I had no idea that he'd been keeping track of how much they'd cost him over the years. But it did bring home for me how much he'd been taking care of them, and it is time for it to stop. You know as well as I what he thought of Blake and his involvement in my father's death."

Blake, Grandda's only living grandchild, had been in more trouble than the few scrapes she'd heard about growing up. And that wasn't even counting his possible responsibility in her dad's hit and run. Great sums of money had been paid to families to keep his name out of the paper and him out of prison. The two times Grandda hadn't paid had been hard on him, he'd told her. And that reason alone was why Blake hated his grandfather so much.

Blake had spent nearly ten years in prison altogether over the course of his life, and hadn't learned anything from his experience. He'd never let Grandda forget how he'd failed him, when in fact, Blake had failed Grandda a great deal more.

Benson had been no different. From the time he'd been about ten, he'd been causing trouble and costing the family money. He'd not been to prison as long as Blake had, just the one time. And even that hadn't taught him a damned thing. Benson, if truth be told, had hurt Grandda more than Blake had because he was the son of his favorite grandchild; her mom, Brooklynn.

"You have invited your mate to this tonight. Do you think he will just let you walk out of his life? And he does know what you are to him, Running Water. There is no way for him not to understand that you are his other half." That was what she was afraid of, that he knew and was right now making plans to order her around. "If you allow him, Darcy can make your life much better than it is now, and he will love you more than you can ever imagine."

It wasn't about loving someone, it was the fact that he, like Morgan, would expect her to do things his way on his schedule. And as much as she loved Morgan, she hated the way that he treated his mate. Lily was a wonderful woman, a great mom and grandma, but to be so subservient to anyone went against every cell in Brooke's body. But Lily seemed to enjoy having to wait on her mate hand and foot, doing everything that he wanted as if she had not a single thought in her head but to do his bidding. And it wasn't just Morgan and his mate, but all

31

couples in the packs and other groups of shifters she'd been around. That sort of life was not for her.

After Morgan left, telling her that he had to make sure things were secure for tonight, she finished her packing and then took a long bubble bath to relax. It was something she did so seldom and wondered why. She decided that she was going to work more bath time into her life. It was fun and she felt really good afterwards.

Taking care with her outfit for tonight, she wondered absently what Darcy would think of how she looked, and dismissed that thought right out of her head. She wasn't going to dress for him or any other man. Besides, he might not even show up. Yeah, she thought, and monkeys would fly right out of her ass. Giggling, she came out of her bedroom to find not just Darcy there, but Morgan as well. Something had happened, she knew it.

"Nothing is wrong." She looked at Darcy when Morgan spoke. "Brody has left the hospital and said that he would contact you later. You knew that he might leave. While Benson is still in his cell, I fear that Blake might come to see you. Darcy has said that he will escort you to the gallery."

She nodded and thought of her poor brother, and not about the handsome man in front of her.

"Yes, he said that he needed to breathe." Darcy took a step toward her, and as much as she wanted to back away from him, she stood her ground. "Morgan said that you're my mate and that you're here to make some demands on me. Well, I won't have it. I have things going well on my own, and I don't need a man in my life fucking it up."

Morgan growled low in his throat and she felt her face heat up. Darcy just laughed and she wanted to hit him. Instead of calling her out on her obvious lie, Darcy smiled and asked her if she was ready to go.

"I am, but I don't need either of you to tell me it's time. I can tell time all by myself." Morgan stood up, shaking his head, and left her alone with Darcy. Feeling her temper get the better of her, she looked at Darcy. "I'm not going to be a slave to you or any other man. I have enough money that I don't need someone to try and take over my life, thinking I need help with things. If I don't know how to do something or can't, I'm able to find someone that can."

"You're very prickly, aren't you? First of all, I'm well aware of how much money you have, as well as your net worth. For the record, I have more, if we're making comparisons. So if you want to blow it all on a shopping spree, which I doubt very much you'd enjoy, then have at it. And I'm the same way. I'd rather do it myself than to have someone lording over me how much more they know than I do." He pulled her into his arms tightly. "As for ordering you about and being my slave, well, that isn't anything that either of us would enjoy. Unless it's to have you tie me to the bed. I think I might enjoy that very much. Lastly, I have no intentions of taking over your life any more than I'd want you to take over mine. We're both adults who know our own selves better than anyone else. However, if you could see your way to let me kiss you, I'd die a happy man right now."

His voice had gone soft, sexy, and full of something she felt all over her body. Like a warm stroke to not just her flesh, but inside too. When he lifted her chin up so that she was able to look into his eyes, she thought that she could see his beautiful cat there. He was as patient and quiet as the man holding her.

"Why do you want to kiss me?" He brushed his mouth over hers, the gentlest of touches, and answered her question with it. Because he needed to. As much as she needed him to kiss her. "You're not going to make me do anything I don't want to."

"No, I'm not. And so you know, I wouldn't have it any other way." He leaned closer to her, and this time, she knew that the kiss that was pending would be all consuming. "May I kiss you, Brooke? Or you can kiss me if you'd like."

"What would be the difference?" She licked her lips and he moaned. "Don't do that. I can feel it."

"As can I. But the difference is, kiss me and we'll find out. Or are you too afraid of what you might feel if you do?"

She pulled his head to hers, closing the gap between them. Just as she pressed her lips to his, she realized that he'd baited her. To show him she was made of sterner stuff, Brooke kissed him with all that she had.

~~~

Darcy nearly regretted his decision to let her have her way in this romance. Because that was what it was going to be for him, an all-out romancing of his mate. But when she wrapped her arms around his neck, holding him to her as she kissed him, Darcy wondered what she'd do if he were to strip her down to nothing and take her right there. When she pulled her mouth from his, Darcy saw hunger in her eyes, felt it in her body, and could smell it on her like expensive perfume. She wanted him almost as much as he did her.

"You are so beautiful, Brooke. And that kiss? That was wonderful. I love the way you feel in my arms and around my body." He shifted her in his arms, pulling her against his cock in a way that she could ride him should she want. "Now it's my turn to kiss you."

He didn't give her a chance to protest, not that he thought she would. So when he leaned his head to hers, his mouth a breath away from her, he watched her tongue as it moved over her lips for him. All Darcy could think about was that this woman was his.

Kissing her was difficult. Not the kissing part, no, never that, but the holding back. He was determined not to rush her, not to force her hand. One thing he'd learned about mates and pushing them too far was that they tended to hurt you, in ways that you'd regret for the rest of your days. But that didn't mean he wasn't going to take all he could from her. Even at the risk of making her angry, he wanted to mark her...but only if she knew what that meant.

Moving his mouth over her chin to her throat, he could taste her need. Her skin was ripe with it, her pulse under his tongue pounding with excitement. When he licked the heated area, knowing that whatever he did now would seal them together, he lifted his head and looked into her eyes.

"You know what I am to you?" She nodded. "I am your mate, forever and a day. From this day forward, where you go, I go. When you hurt, I hurt. When you need me, for whatever reason, I'll be standing beside you."

"I won't be ordered around." He told her he'd never do that. "You will. You'll make me do things, things that will benefit you and not me."

"I won't do that to you." He watched her face. "But I can see that you don't believe me. That's all right for now. But I want you to know that for as long as you and I live, I will never expect or want you to do anything that you don't want to. I swear this to you on my life."

Pulling away from her, holding her steady, not just for her but for himself, Darcy moved back from her. Until she understood him better, trusted him with all that she was, he wouldn't take what was not freely offered. He might be hurting right now, but he wasn't going to be a bastard about

35

having her as his mate. Brooke already had a poor opinion of mates in general, and he wasn't adding to it.

"May I escort you to the gallery?" It took her several seconds to answer him, and when she did, he smiled. Nodding, she took his arm when he offered it to her. He wanted to take her into them, not have her hold onto him as she did now. Deciding that he would change the subject, he spoke of the gallery and what he'd seen on the way here. "There was a line of people waiting to get in when I drove by a bit ago. You're going to have a nice show."

"You won't tell them who I am, will you? I can't let anyone know." He assured her that he'd not do that, hurt that she'd think he would. "Good. And so you know, I have no idea what game you're playing now, but I'm not going to cave. I can't have you in my life."

"It's a bit too late for that, I think. But I'm not playing any games with you. Until you trust me, which I can tell that you don't, I'm only going to be here for you." He let the doors seal around them in the elevator before turning to her. "I'm a man of my word. And until you ask me to take this relationship to the next stage—because never doubt that this is a relationship between us—I'll wait. Maybe not as patiently as I should, but I'll not rush you in any way."

When the doors opened to the lobby of her hotel, he put out his arm again. He was determined now to make sure that he could touch her in any way that he could. Maybe it wasn't fair of him, but he had to give himself this, if nothing else. As they walked to the waiting limo out front, he talked about how he and Mac had had lunch at the North Market and done some Christmas shopping as well.

Darcy knew that she was off balance...he was as well. But he was enjoying the look of confusion on her face, probably a bit more than he should have. The way she kept biting her lip as if she was trying to figure him out wasn't helping much, but he had a goal now and he was going to stick to it, even if it killed him...which he was sort of afraid it would. But Darcy kept up an easy flow of conversation, asking her if she'd started shopping yet.

"I do it all online. There are a lot of places in town I guess I could go to, but I don't leave the mountain much." He asked her how far it was to town. "Depends on if you mean the touristy one or the area the locals use. There are a lot of outlet places just beyond the circle of tourist shops. I shop there if I have to go somewhere. I get a lot of the gifts for the pack at a store that specializes in outdoor items."

"I think Mac and I read about that one. When I leave soon, I'm going to have to check it out. My parents have this cook that loves to use cast iron. She and her husband camp when they go on vacations and use them there as well. I need to pick up some things for Mom to give as gifts. So you'll need to tell me where the outlet places are so I can go." She looked out the window and Darcy smiled. "I would imagine you hate to leave your home. There must be a lot of good memories for you there, despite your grandfather no longer being with you."

"Yes. My great grandda built the house—well, the first part of it—when he married my great grandma. She wasn't thrilled with having a log cabin without much in the way of heat or electricity, I guess. Great Grandda told me that sometimes, in the winter, they'd sleep in the pottery shed, as it was a good deal warmer than the house when he was running whatever mode of kiln he had. Then my grandfather came along, and he lived there with his own wife when they were first married too. She was a great deal less happy with the conditions than Great Grandma was, so the house was added onto and updated. Then my Uncle Blake and Mom were born." He asked her what happened to her grandparents. "My grandma left Grandda when he was hurt. I'm not sure how the accident happened, something about a fishing trip, but he wasn't able to get around very well after it. He'd lost his leg, or a portion of it, when he fell through some ice. She got sick of being around someone that got more attention than she did was the way Great Grandda told it."

Darcy was surprised at how much of her life had been a series of bad relationships; her grandparents, parents, and even her siblings. When she continued about her uncle, mom, and dad, he decided that he might be in deeper than he thought.

"Uncle Blake wasn't ever a very nice person. When he and my mom were younger, he'd beat her pretty badly when there was no one around. My grandda, who was raising Mom and Uncle Blake as best he could, would just ignore him. But Great Grandda would beat his ass and then some. When my mom met my dad, William Graceson—how I got my middle name, by the way—she tried to keep him away from the house before they were wed so that Blake would never find out about them. They were married in secret, but because of her affiliation with the art world, she kept her last name. And then when Benson was born, they went to live with my grandfather. I was born there, in the big house, and so was Brody. But just days before he was born, my dad was killed in an accident. It was a hit and run. There had been a break-in at the pottery shop that Great Grandda had in town, and it was thought that my dad had found the man there and had run after him. When the police arrived at the scene, my dad was lying in the street with his neck broken and the car long gone. And as far as we know, it was never found. His death was too much for my mom, and after Brody was born, she passed away too."

The limo had stopped some time into her story, but he didn't say anything, nor had the door opened to disturb her. Darcy watched her sitting there, her tears going unchecked down her cheeks hurting him right over his heart. When she turned to him finally, he asked her if she needed a few minutes, and she turned to the window again.

"I'll be all right in a few minutes. I just.... With my grandda gone, I feel so alone without Brody around, and my things. I think that's why I need to go home so badly. I need to feel close to them." He understood that. It's why he went to his parents' home as much as he could. "You must think I'm a silly girl for being this upset about missing an old man."

"No, I don't think you're silly at all. You have lost a great deal in your life. I'm sorry about your childhood and the way you were treated by those that should have loved you." Brooke nodded. "And I'm terribly sorry about your parents, and grandparents as well. You've lost a lot more than most people I know."

"They're all on my mountain." When she turned to him then, Darcy saw that she'd hardened something inside of her. He was sure she was trying her best to block him, keep him from getting into a place in her heart that had been broken enough. "I'm leaving when this is done tonight. And when I do, I don't want you to contact me again."

Darcy said nothing as he lifted his hand and rapped twice on the barrier between them and the driver. When the door was opened and he was let out, he waited there, putting his hand inside the dark roomy area and hoping that she'd take it. When she did, he helped her out but stopped her from moving past him to the building. She looked up at him when he put his hand around her small waist.

"You're my mate. If you leave tonight, so do I. You can

let me stay with you on your mountain, or I'll take a place in town. Either way, I'm not going away. I won't hurt you or force you, but I'm going to be where you are. I need to make sure you're safe, and I don't think you will be so as long as your uncle and brother are around."

Putting out his arm again, he was sure she wasn't going to take it. Her anger at him nearly seared Darcy when she glared at him. Darcy wanted to smile, even to laugh at her, but he didn't. And when she walked by him, not taking his arm, he nearly laughed again. But the view he had of her now, the one of her walking away, was worth her not taking his arm.

Her feet were encased in the sexiest shoes he'd ever seen. High heels, dark and shiny, with just enough sparkle to perfectly match the dress she wore. So when she took the first step up into the gallery, her anger making her step a little less carefully than he was sure she normally would, he leapt to her aid when she started to go down. He held her in his arms until she looked up at him.

"I nearly fell." Darcy said he had her. She stared at him, her eyes filling with tears as he did so. "I can't change for you, Darcy. I just can't."

"And I don't want you to. I know you don't believe me, but I have no desire to have you do anything that you don't want to. My life, it's whatever you need for me to be. Not the other way around. I promise you." She asked him what his family would say. "That they're happy I am happy. And that you are."

As they moved up the rest of the stairs without any more slips, he said remained silent. She was digesting, that was all he could think to call it. Every part of her face said that she didn't believe him. Even her posture, stiff with some anger, told him so. But he was going to make this work for her, even

40

if it was the last thing he did. And he was pretty sure it might well kill him before this was over.

Darcy was both surprised and anxious about seeing his family in the gallery. His dad hugged him like he'd not seen him for a month rather than the few days he'd been gone. His mom hugged him as well, but she was eyeing Brooke to see if she might fit in with them. Darcy introduced her to his family, saying only that her first name was Brooke, but they knew who she was, and it looked as if they knew what she was to him. He supposed Mac had made a few calls, and that was what had brought them down this way. He wondered who he'd have to thank for getting them together. He thought it might have been Riordan or Storm, but wasn't sure just yet.

"Right nice work you have here, darling. I'm betting you work pretty hard at getting these things all lined up for something like this." Brooke looked at him, then at his dad when he continued. "I bet old Daniel, he'd be really proud of you about now. I've heard nothing but excitement about what these folks are here to see."

"He was. Most of the work here is his. It was one of the last things he did, picking out the pieces to come here for this show." Dad asked her to show them around. Brooke looked at him. "You told them."

"No. I told you, Nikki is a good cop and she found out. And if you tell them, which I'm sure they've already figured out that you don't want others to know who you are, they'll keep your secret as well as I will." She said nothing. "Show my dad and mom around, and then we'll talk if you want. But whatever you decide to do, I'll be right here."

"I'm not going to let you do this to me. I've been threatened before." He jerked her to his body, his temper getting the better of him for a moment. "Are you going to hit me?"

41

"No. Kiss you." He did too, with all the passion that he could. When he let her go, holding her until she could stand on her own feet, he kissed her on the nose before backing away. "My family is waiting."

As soon as they were in the next room, Darcy let out a long breath. When someone standing next to him laughed, he only glanced at Storm when she asked him if he was all right. He told her he wasn't sure yet.

"Yeah, I can see that. She's not in the best of humor right now. What did you do to her? Or should I ask you, what didn't you do to her?" He told her what his plan was. "Okay. I can see that. It would be a first in this family, a male using romance instead of sex to get their mate. But I have to tell you, she's going to be a really hard shell to crack. I found some other things about her you might want to take into consideration."

"Her brother or the uncle?" Storm told him it was both. "Blake, he's hurt her, hasn't he? And recently."

"Yes. About a week before her grandda died, she spent a few hours in the emergency room. Brody called the cops when he found her right outside the shop, Running Waters, unconscious and bleeding. It's believed that someone drugged her. But all she told the authorities was that she'd been in a deep cave and wasn't entirely sure how she'd gotten there. But whatever had happened, she was hurt pretty badly when Brody found her. Nineteen stitches in just her head alone. Bruises, as well as scrapes. The police don't know if it was Blake or Benson. But both of them have done it before. Hurt her, I mean."

"Did she press charges the other times they hurt her?" Storm told him usually, but she thought with her grandda being so ill, she might have let them have a pass on that last time. "She's going to leave tonight for her mountain. I'm going as well. She's not terribly thrilled about that, as you can tell, but I can't leave her now."

"We thought you'd say that, and one of them drove your truck down and packed a few things in it for you." He thanked her. "Don't thank me yet. I also put a team on her mountain for you, and a few others around the shop and town. There's a pack there, the Boyer pack. They were hard to convince that we only meant to help. I think they have taken her as one of their own. Anyway, once your name was mentioned, the doors were opened for us to help them. And that's all we're doing for now, helping."

He told her about Morgan and the night that he'd had to subdue Benson. He moved into the next room where they were as Brooke talked about the piece that stood just behind her. Darcy was afraid that she was going to be hurt by her family, more than they had already done.

"Will you keep an eye on things for me? I have some contractors coming in this week to do some of the floors in the hotel." She said that she and the rest would. He turned to her. "I would also like for you to find me everything and anything you can about her uncle and brother."

"It's on the front seat of your truck. Also what I could find on her and the other brother, Brody. You owe me big time." Darcy grinned at her. "Use that charm on her, not me. I'm going to love watching her come to terms with you."

He hoped it turned out well. Right now, all he could think about was that she wasn't going to be any happier with him now than when he showed up on her mountain. Darcy thought he might just enjoy her getting pissed off.

CHAPTER 3

There it was again...the sound of something ringing in the air. Climbing out of bed, she pulled on pants and a too big sweatshirt. Brooke went out to the porch and watched the man chopping wood. He'd been at it a while too, if the sweat rolling off his naked back was any indication. Then there was the neatly stacked timber next to him. Brooke thought that he even made being sweaty look like a chocolate cake with lots of icing. Storming down to where he was working, she wanted to both lick him and throw some of the wood at him at the same time.

"What the hell are you doing?" He paused in bringing the heavy axe down and looked at her. When he let it go, the log that was on the stump not just split in two, but fell away from the stump two feet or more. "I asked you a question. What are you doing here? And for that matter, what the hell are you doing chopping wood that no one asked you to? Did you follow me, is that what you did to find this place?"

"No. If you remember, you left without telling me. Sneaky of you, but I figured it out. And finding you, that part wasn't as easy as I thought it would be. Well, that's not quite true...I knew you'd be off the grid, I just never thought of how much." The axe came down on the next length of wood and shattered under his strength. "As for chopping the wood? I'm cutting it

45

because you need it. I talked to Morgan—who was nice enough to help me get here, by the way—and he said that I could make myself useful and help out with the wood splitting. I've never done this before."

She didn't believe that. The precision with which he was hitting those logs was outstanding. And he made it look effortless. Brooke couldn't even lift the heavy axe up enough to bring it down, much less have what it took to make the log look like he'd pulverized it with a single blow.

She watched him split four more logs before he turned and grinned at her. A part of her wanted to smack him in the head, while the rest of her, the insane part, wanted to go to where a small trickle of sweat moved by his nipple and see if he tasted as good as he looked right now. When he set the axe down and leaned on it, she had a feeling that he knew what she was thinking, and it pissed her off.

"You're not staying here. I don't know what you think to accomplish by showing up uninvited, but you can just go home now." He said nothing but stood there. "Did you hear me? I said for you to go home."

"I am home."

The axe was picked up again and laid on his shoulder while he bent and picked up another log. Christ, the man had an ass that made her want to rub her hands and every other part of her all over it. When he set the log on the stump, she wanted to stomp her foot and scream at him to just get it over with. What she wanted done, Brooke wasn't sure...but she wanted it done. Instead of arguing with an obvious idiot, she went back into her house and started pulling things from the cabinets to make breakfast. She hated to cook, but figured she needed her strength to deal with him.

"If he thinks he's going to be sleeping here, then he's as

fruity as the man that lives in the shack on the hill."

Mr. Coulter was a nice man, but he saw ghosts and thought that the revenuers were out to get him. The big still in his backyard that he had used to make moonshine hadn't been run in ten years, but that didn't stop him from worrying about it.

She was pouring pancakes on the old cast iron griddle when the door opened behind her. Darcy had looked good down by the wood pile, but this close he looked like she could have enjoyed him for every meal. Dessert too. Turning her back to him when he asked her if he could get a glass of water, Brooke's imagination took a dirty turn. Christ, the things she could do with a bottle of water, a few ropes, and this man.

"There's water in the fridge in the shed." He opened the refrigerator next to her and she stared as he took one of the many bottles in the fridge, and after opening it, tilted it up to his mouth.

It was just a drink, her mind told her. There was no reason whatsoever to find the way his Adam's apple moved up and down sexy. The way condensation dripped on his chest wasn't a reason for her to want to chase it with her tongue. And she could think of no sane reason to wonder if the hand holding the bottle would hold her breast the same way, a gentle but firm grip while he suckled at her. She looked at him when he said her name.

"I don't know what's wrong with me." He nodded, as if he knew and wasn't sharing with her. "I think I'm all hot and bothered by you because it's been a long time since I've dated. Don't you think that's it? I do. I think that's it."

"I don't know; is that what you think or want to think?" She nodded, then shook her head. "Yeah, I didn't think it was that either. Could it be that you're all hot and bothered because you simply want me?"

"I don't want you." He just nodded and told her that her pancakes were ready. Turning them over and putting them on a plate, she handed it to him when he said nothing more. "I'm not going to let you be a part of my life. And if I need relief, then I'll find it on my own."

"You do that. But if you don't mind, I'd really like to watch if you're going to use a vibrator. I know you've not had sex before, I can smell you. And anyway, if another man touches you with the intent of giving you relief, I'll kill him. But watching you use one of those on yourself…well, I can't tell you what sort of things come to mind right now." He sat down with the plate of pancakes. He'd gotten out the syrup too, as well as the tub of butter she loved, while she'd been musing over his body, apparently. And when he got up and went to the fridge again, she turned back to her task. But all her mind could center on was having him watch her as she brought herself to climax with her toy.

"Orange juice?" She asked him what he meant. "To drink. Would you like me to pour you a glass of orange juice? I see you have tea as well, but I didn't know if it was sweet or not."

"No. I don't care for sweet tea, hot or…. I don't understand why you're here. And chopping my wood. I can hire someone to do that for me." He poured her a glass of tea and then himself. She put her plate on the table after turning off the stove, and stared at him. "Why are you doing this? Do you think to wear me down? It won't work. I've been alone for a long time, and am made of better stuff than that."

"I believe you. But the reason I'm here? For a great many reasons, I guess. First of all, you know that I'm your mate, so that's not going to cut it with you, I guess. But more importantly, I'm here because I need to be. Same reasons, but not all of it."

48

He handed her a napkin and she took it as he continued. "Your uncle bailed Benson out of jail this morning. I wasn't sure if you'd been made aware of that or not. And while they can't get here today, something about his car and it being impounded until Monday, they will be soon enough. And neither of them are very happy at the moment. But then, since I don't know them, that could be a normal state for them."

"It is. Especially where I'm concerned. But that doesn't explain why you're here." He nodded and moaned when he took a bite of pancakes. Brooke felt it all the way to her toes and back twice when he did it again with the second bite. "Stop doing that. I'm trying to talk to you and you're not making it easy."

"You have no idea how uneasy I am just sitting here with you, knowing that you're naked beneath those clothes you have on. And having an idea that you just tumbled out of your bed and pulled them on to come down to where I was to yell at me. By the way, when you're excited, your nipples poke against the material." She felt her face heat up as she pulled her sweatshirt from her chest. "I can almost imagine how you look naked. Not all of you, but enough to know that you have an amazing body and full breasts. And I can smell you. You might hate it, but you're aroused and wet."

"We're not having sex." He nodded and ate two more bites of his breakfast, but didn't moan again. Brooke wasn't sure if that was good or not. "How do you know about...? Nikki again."

"No, this time I heard from my brother, Aedan. He's the state governor for Ohio. Right now it's just a fill in job until the election, but I'm pretty sure that he's going to be there for a bit." She nodded, then shook her head. Brooke was beginning to feel like she'd fallen down the long rabbit hole. "I'll make another batch. These are really good. You should talk to Andi. She has this recipe for pancakes with apples in them. Wow, they're good."

He got up and filled the griddle with more pancake batter after it was hot enough. He had danced water on the grill to check the temperature first, and that impressed her. But she didn't want to be impressed by him. She wanted him to go away and leave her alone.

When her phone rang she got up to answer it, thinking of ways to murder Darcy. Or to get him to take her to the bedroom just up the stairs from where they were. It took her a moment to realize that she wasn't paying attention to the caller, and that they were pissed off.

"I'm sorry, what did you say?" She knew who it was then…Uncle Blake, and he wasn't just pissed, he was furious. "What are you talking about?"

"I said…do you know how much I fucking hate you at this moment? I said that we've got an attorney and we're suing your ass. You fucking did this to us, and now you're going to fucking pay." She looked at Darcy when he took the phone from her. But she could still hear Uncle Blake, and didn't want to take the phone back to tell him that she'd done nothing at all to him. He'd brought this all on himself. "When I'm finished with you, Brooke, you're not going to have shit. Do you hear me? Nothing but one of those fucking ugly pots that you make. And even then, I'm going to make sure that it's broken."

"And how do you propose to do that?" Darcy didn't sound angry but amused. She wanted to tell him all he was going to do was piss Blake off more, but she sat down when Darcy pulled the chair out for her. "I see. And this attorney you've hired, have you told him that you're broke, that you don't even have the retainer? Or for that matter, a case? I'm to understand that there was great detail in the will as to why you were left without anything. I myself think it's about time, but you can't go against family. Unless they're worthless pieces of shit like you are."

Brooke laid her head on the table, pushing the food away, no longer hungry. Uncle Blake would haunt her for the rest of her days if she didn't give him what he wanted. But she had a feeling that once she started trying to keep him in the way that he wanted, he'd never have enough. Not until she was as broke as he was. She looked at Darcy when he said her name.

"He's not going to hurt you. Financially, nor physically. Not so long as I have breath in my body." She nodded but said nothing. "I'm going to have my brothers look into a few things for you, all right?"

"Uncle Blake is blaming me for something, right? I never quite caught what it was. I don't suppose he told you, did he?" He told her. "I see. Not really, but I don't understand how Benson having an unfit car to drive is my fault. I didn't wreck it, nor did I tell him to drive it up to Ohio to come after me. Why would anyone else care for that matter?"

"I don't know, love, but in my experience, people who are desperate say stupid things. And the car was an issue. Nikki said that it had no door on the driver's side, as well as one of the tires was just a spare, one of those little ones. Plus, the windshield was broken and he wasn't going to be able to see out of it to drive." She nodded and took the fork when he handed it to her. Her plate was in front of her as well. "You have to eat something. Letting yourself get weak and sick is only going to make it worse."

"He really hates me." Darcy wisely said nothing. "I don't suppose you'll just go home and leave me to this, will you? I mean, you've talked to him. He's going to take his anger at me

51

having it all out on you now too."

"He can try. But no, I'm not leaving you. Especially after talking to him. I don't think he's going to simply go away, do you?" Darcy stood up and stretched. She saw his cat as he seemed to race along his body. "When you look at me like that, it's all I can do to hold my cat. He wants to show himself to you. We need for you to see us in the event that when your brother and uncle get here, you don't freak out."

"I never freak out. Not normally." He took his shirt off and tossed it on the chair. When he opened the top snap to his pants, she felt herself start to panic. "Do you have to do that? Be naked, I mean? Now?"

"I have some extra clothing, but it's at my hotel. If I shift dressed like this, I'm not going to have anything to put on. I'd have to be naked until I could get something to put on. Would that bother you?" She had no idea how to answer that, so just watched him as he pulled his pants off. "Don't run."

~~~

If she stared at his cock much more, Darcy wasn't sure what he might do. Letting his cat take him, he tried to breathe through his mouth, trying to lessen the scent of her arousal, but all it did was make him taste her need. Christ, she was going to kill him if he didn't get some control.

"Can you hear me?" He nodded and laid his head on her lap, and she smacked him, making him jerk away from her. "You bastard. You tell me not to run, and that's all I can think to do. You might have mentioned that you're fucking huge."

Her face heated up and he smiled to himself. She had noticed, was all he could think about. When she stood up, knocking him off her lap when he laid his head back on it, he sat down and watched her pace. She did this like she did everything else, he noticed…with determination and purpose.

52

"I'm assuming that since we've never exchanged blood, we can't communicate either." He only stared at her; she knew more than he thought she might, for which he was grateful. "Okay, so I get to talk all I want and you have to listen to me. Good. I like this way even better. I don't want you in my life. Not now, not ever. But you've just barged your way in, haven't you?"

He wasn't sure he could have answered that even if he was able to speak to her. Darcy wasn't sure where she was going with this...barging in wasn't something that he'd wanted to happen. Well, sort of not wanted. He had shown up here unannounced, and he did want to be in her life, but not by forcing her. When he realized that he should be paying attention to her, she smacked him again. This time he grabbed her hand in his mouth before she could take it back. Biting down just enough to draw blood, he let her go and stood there while she held her hand to her body.

Okay, for starters, I did not barge into your life. We met because my sister-in-law bought some tickets for my brother and his wife. Fate brought us together. She sat down and he put his head back on her lap. *I can smell you. You want me as much as I do you, admit it.*

"I want to have sex with you, yes. It's about all I can think about." He liked that and nearly told her so when she spoke again. "But it's not going to happen, Darcy. We live in two different worlds. I like to be alone, in my home here, and work in my shed. You have a loud, wonderful family that is noisy and touchy. I'm not into touchy feely stuff."

There are times when they're too much for me too. It's why I live in a hotel, alone. I'm taking my time renovating it so that no one expects me to fill it with people. She asked him why he'd gotten a hotel if he didn't want to fill it. *It was for sale and I'm trying to*

53

help revitalize the downtown area. And it's a good sound investment.

"That's not an explanation. Not to mention a poor excuse for hiding out. At least I'm honest about why I want to be alone." He asked her why. "Because people suck. And if you do find someone that you wouldn't mind spending some time with, they burn you. Even if they're related to you, they burn you."

Who? She put her hand on his head and rubbed him behind the ears. He knew that she was doing it without thinking. Because if she knew how she was making him feel, he was pretty sure she'd hit him harder than she had already. *Who burned you, Brooke? Besides your brother and uncle?*

"My grandda's secretary has threatened to go to the newspapers and tell them who I am. Who my grandda and mom were as well. Darcy, I don't understand why I feel like I can talk to you about things and.... You never seem to judge me, do you? I mean, I think if I told you that I murdered someone and got rid of their body in a kiln, you'd more than likely say they probably deserved it." He told her that they would have. "See? You're not right in the head. No one should be able to commit murder and anyone think it was all right."

I think, and you might not agree with me, but sometimes you're given no choice in the matter. Kill or be killed. People can only take being pushed so far before they snap. And I also think that it's not always as simple as that. There are people who do put themselves into positions to make it look like they'd had no choice. They murder so that whatever agenda they had can be justified in the eyes of others. She asked him who had done that to him. *Not to me. But I've heard my sisters talking. Nikki and Storm, you've met them. You know what they do for a living, or did, and know that there are times when they've run into this. As you've pointed out, people suck.*

He watched her, feeling her fingers running through his

fur. Listened to her heart beating, slow and steady now. Darcy could almost hear her thoughts, the way she was weighing each and every one of them as they circled around. When she looked down at him, he wasn't the least bit surprised at her question.

"What do we do now?" He licked the hand laying in her lap. And when she shifted on the seat, Darcy moved deeper between her legs and rested his head right over her pussy. This time when she moved, opening her legs wider for him, he nudged them wider still and buried his nose over her heat. "I could come right now. Thinking of your cock naked like you were before your cat took you. Christ, I need to come so badly."

Take off your pants. He didn't think she would, and in a way hoped that she wouldn't. This wasn't the direction that he wanted to take with her right now. But his need for her, her scent perfuming the air, made him needy, painfully so. *He wants to taste you. Lick your pussy until you come for us both.*

When she pulled them off, never standing up, his cat purred loudly as he tasted her, licking her as best he could the way she sat. Christ, she was wet. And delicious. And when she cried out, her climax making her bow up off the seat, Darcy had his cat move in closer, wrapping his tongue around her clit and nipping at it until she cried out that she was coming a second, then a third time. When she stood up and called him, Darcy took his body back and stood up as well.

"I want to blame you for this, but I won't. I can't. I need you as badly as I think you do me." He said nothing. "You'll hurt me, Darcy, I know it. But there is nothing I can do about it now."

He knew that she felt this way, not just about him but everyone. They'd hurt her and she fully expected him to do the same. But he wouldn't, not if he could help it. He wanted her to be happy and safe. And even though his body told him to take her, in his heart, he could not.

"I won't have you going into this with mistrust between us, Brooke. I need you to believe me when I tell you I won't change you, anything about you." She said nothing but took his hand in hers. He pulled back, probably the hardest thing he'd ever done. "As much as I'd like to take you to your room and make love to you all night long, I can't do it. Not like this. Not with you thinking the things that you are."

"Why not? I'm willing. Needy. And I can see that you are." His cock jumped, the pre-cum leaking from the tip in long streams. "Just fuck me and we'll be mates. I'm sure that was what you knew was going to happen the moment you set foot on my mountain anyway. Why are you suddenly acting like this isn't what you planned all along?"

He hurt with her words. They were like daggers being driven into his chest. Reaching for his pants, he pulled them on and then grabbed his shirt. He was out the door before she could say another word. And not slamming the door was harder than he thought it would be.

Going to the wood pile again, he picked up the axe he'd discarded earlier to see what she was doing in the house. He was still holding it on his shoulder when he saw the big wolf just outside the ring of trees around the property. He and Morgan had exchanged blood just this morning, so conversation was easy between the two of them. It was the subject matter that had him talking now.

"She's pissed off at me. I'm not entirely sure why, but she's pretty mad." Morgan said nothing but did sit down. Putting the axe down, Darcy sat as well, facing the beautiful home. "When she told me that her great grandda had built this house, a log cabin she said, I have no idea why, but I expected it to be this hobbled together place with a couch on the front lawn and about a dozen dead cars all over. I know that's stereotyping, but I just didn't know what to expect."

Her great great grandfather was a very good man, and he knew a great deal about many things. He built many of the cabins in this area, or had a hand in them being built. As well as doing a lot of his own work around the homestead, such as bringing in water from the streams and getting the required permits to get electricity to his home. He was a man who knew what the future would hold, I think. The front of the house, what he thought was the original log cabin, had been bigger than he'd imagined as well. But the additions made the house look like it not only had been here forever, but blended well into the mountain and trees that surrounded it. *It's said that when Peter, her great great grandfather, set his mind on something, there was little to deter him. So when his son, Daniel, asked for his help in putting his home up, he did it with the same mindset as he did everything. Done well and with thought to the years it would still be standing here. As well as the families that it would protect.*

"Brooke sounds like she took after him a great deal." Morgan agreed. "I don't know a lot about building. I've been doing some of my own work on an empty hotel that I purchased a few weeks back. But this place, it's built like it was meant to stay long after man has decided to move away."

It was tall too, enough for the two stories that he knew it needed to accommodate a man of his height. The wrap around porch incorporated into the new part of the house was deep, and the railing around it was made with all different kinds of woods, including oak and maple as well as redwood. This was a porch meant to sit on and enjoy the view. And even though he'd only been in the kitchen, he'd bet anything that it had one hell of a view.

The rest of the house, the newer part, had been built on the back of the existing house. It was another story taller, and about four times bigger than the cabin had been. Chimneys graced both ends of the additions, and the stone that made them had more than likely been found in the yard and surrounding area. Then it had been stacked in a way that was both functional as well as artistic, just as the people who had built it wanted it to be. Even the house proper had been built with the nature around it in mind. He could see windows now that were tall, as well as wide, on either side of the front door and along the side of the house. Shutters too, the kind that were functional, not just pretty decorations.

When the door to the house opened, Darcy looked at Brooke when she came out and made her way to the shed.

"Why is it called a shed?" Morgan laughed and Darcy did as well. "I mean, shed makes you think a small, one roomed building with so much junk in it that it defies reasoning as to why someone would save it all. But that place she works in, it's as big, if not bigger than, my parents' home."

Her great grandfather, Daniel, he called his place a shed, the one before this one. Which I suppose it really was. It stood in the same place for a great many years before it became apparent that he needed to grow with her. When Running Water came to work with him, even as a small child, I think he believed she'd need more. He told me once that he thought her to be better than him. Darcy had seen both their work, and had to admit that even he found that to be true. *However, I would never say that to her. Not to her face at any rate.*

When Morgan stood up, his fur standing on end, Darcy stood as well. His cat was there, running along his skin, telling him in his own way, that he was ready for whatever was coming. When the beat up truck pulled into the drive, Darcy stayed where he was, but picked up the large axe again. Whatever this threat was, if it was one, he was going to be ready for it.

Don't kill him, but be wary of him. While he is not overly dangerous, he is a man who is slightly off in his head at times. Mostly about Running Water. Darcy asked Morgan who he was. *A man that thinks that young Running Water should forget playing with mud and join him in his home. To be honest, I'm not sure why he wishes that, but he does. He has been telling anyone that would listen that he is going to wed her and live in her big house. Oh, and he also has a desire to have all the wild animals on the mountain shot. I have no idea how he hopes to accomplish such a feat. Most of us can shoot better than him.*

Darcy thanked him for the advice and information, and headed to the truck. He neither put on his shirt nor put down the axe. It was time to show this man that while he'd not mated with her as yet, and might not ever if she had her way, there was no poaching on his woman. He glanced at the shed when he heard the door open and slam shut. Or maybe, he thought when he got a look at Brooke's face, he'd just let her take care of the man.

CHAPTER 4

Thomas saw Brooke before he saw the man. But when he did, he wondered if he should come back another day. Christ, he was fucking huge, and that axe in his hand looked decidedly medieval. Putting out his hand to try and be friendly to the man, he jerked it behind his back when it was slapped. Brooke was glaring at him. Again.

"Now honey, I was just trying to make his acquaintance. It's right nice of you to hire someone to come and chop up the wood. But I told you that I'd get to it." He looked at the man then back at Brooke when she said nothing. "You paying him well, I hope?"

"Like what I pay or don't pay someone is any of your fucking business. And if I waited on you to do anything, if I was ever inclined to ask you to help me, there would be nothing done. What are you doing here now? I thought I made it perfectly clear that I didn't want you coming around anymore."

Thomas smiled at her. She was pretty when she was all riled up like this, but no matter what his momma said, he didn't think Brooke was ever gonna marry him.

"God save me from men and their need to be helpful."

"Now honey, don't be—"

He'd forgotten about calling her honey. Thomas knew as

surely as he was standing there that she was going to light into
him again. So when she hit him in the face with her fist, he held
onto his truck door so as not to hit the ground and muddy his
pants again. He hated being dirty, and lately it seemed that
someone was forever messing him up. Neat and tidy, that was
the only way he liked it.

"Don't call me honey. I've told you a thousand times, I'm
not bee shit. Nor am I anything to you that you should be using
endearments. I've told you again and again, Thomas, I'm not
going to go out with you, I'm not going to marry you, and I am
most certainly not going to let you live in my house. No matter
what your momma has told you. How many times do I have
to tell you that for it to sink in?" Thomas nodded and looked at
the man who wasn't trying to hold back his laughter one bit. It
was sort of rude of him to be listening in on their little spat, and
he told him that. "We are not having a spat, Thomas. I'm mad
that you keep coming here with only one thing coming out
of your mouth. No. Just no, to whatever errand your momma
has sent you to try on me again. You are not *ever* going to be
anything to me."

Thomas wanted to cry. But he looked at the big man and
tried to salvage some of his pride. He didn't have much of it of
late, but he had to make this work with Brooke. His momma
was getting frustrated with him.

"She's a little peeved at me." The big man only cocked a
brow at him. "She gets that way when I call her pretty names.
Only woman I've ever met that didn't care to be called hon...
didn't like being called sweet names."

"I'm thinking you shouldn't be talking about her as if
she's not here, Thomas. That doesn't seem to be making her
any happier with you than calling her honey. Brooke might
just hit you again." Thomas covered his nose and wondered

if she really would hit him. She didn't hit like a girl either, but a man, and he'd have to talk to Momma about that. "Besides the whole endearment thing, I think you might have it wrong about her being *peeved* at you. I'm pretty sure that she's royally pissed off."

"Oh no. I've given her no reason to be that way at me. It's just the way we do things. She gets upset with me and I tell her I'm sorry and we go on again. I even brought her some flowers like I usually do." Brooke started toward him with a glint that he wasn't sure about in her eye. But the big man grabbed her around the waist and lifted her up so that she couldn't touch him. Thomas was sort of glad for it. He had a feeling that she wasn't gonna give him a kiss, like his momma told him to get, to let him know she was sorry for her treatment of him, but might have been set on hurting him again. There was no predicting what this woman would do when her mind was in a snit. When she was set back down on her feet, Thomas felt better and looked at the man still holding the axe.

If Thomas was honest with himself, which Momma told him wasn't a good thing, he'd think that the stranger looked good standing there like he was. He cut a fine picture, as his daddy used to say when he'd see a pretty woman. Thomas thought he'd like to have his name. Just to tell his momma.

"Who might you be? I mean, if you're going to be working here, not that I really want a stranger around when I'm not here, but I should know your name, don't you think?" He told him and Thomas wasn't impressed enough to try and remember it. After he had a little talk with Brooke about hiring strangers, Darcy would be gone soon enough. And his momma would be really proud of him for thinking of getting him off the land.

Darcy wrapped his arm around her waist after she told Thomas that she'd hire who she wanted. To be honest, Brooke looked ready to nail him again, but the big man only told her to behave.

"Well, Dawson, you get on back to work now. That wood ain't gonna chop itself, I'm thinking. I'll be having a little conversation with my intended here, and then I'll come and talk to you."

"His name is Darcy, not Dawson, you moron. And he is not the hired help. He's.... He is...." Brooke looked at Dawson, or whatever his name was, and she looked confused when she turned back to him. "It's not important what he is, but whatever it is, it's none of your business. I've asked you several times not to come back here, and to stop telling everyone that I'm going to marry you. As I have told you, again, and again, I am never ever going to marry you, Thomas, and I'm never going to fall in love with you."

Thomas shook his head, trying to think what he was to do now. Then it hit him. Poor girl was still grieving, he guessed, and he decided that it was time for him to make his final stand with her. She needed him. It might take her a bit to realize that, but he was a patient man. Just as soon as she agreed to marry him, he'd give her all the time in the world to come to the same conclusion as he had about them. They were meant to be together, his momma said.

Thomas had been living with his momma ever since his first marriage had fallen apart. He'd wanted to explain things to Becca, his wife, but she wasn't having it. And when she'd gone to his momma and told her what had been going on behind her back, Thomas had had to move in with Momma again and give up the pretty little house that he'd gotten before Becca had agreed to marry him. He'd been living in shame since then. His momma had told him he had better marry Brooke and make people forget what he'd done to poor little Becca.

"I was wondering when you and I could go into town and look at rings. You know, when I was here the last time, you and I never fixed that up. I know old Mr. Gravely, and so you know he told me if I could get you to agree to come in and look at them, he'd give us a good discount. Might even give me the ring if you were to just say yes about marrying me where he could hear you. I think that's worth the trip, don't you?" Brooke crossed her arms over her chest and he felt his face heat. She wasn't wearing any undergarments again. "Brooke, hon.... Brooke, you should go in and dress properly. I don't care for those pant things that you wear, but I know that you have to be comfortable to do your crafts. But being underdressed like you are, showing some of your more...girly parts, gives men the wrong impression."

"Girly parts? And crafts? You think what she does for a living is crafts? Like arts and crafts kids do in school?" David... what was his name again? No matter...David seemed to be surprised by what she did, and he started to explain to him how she worked with dirt all day, but he cut him off. "She's a potter. A very talented and artistic one who has works of art all over the world. You cannot equate what she does to something so simple as crafts. I mean, come on, have you seen her work?"

"No. I see no reason to bother with it. Once we're wed, which will be soon, Momma said she'll give all that up to be the wife that I need to make a man of me. You'll see. Momma is never wrong." Daniel looked at Brooke, then at him as Thomas continued. "I would allow her to do it some. I mean, it does seem to make her feel good to be doing it. But not on the scale that she is now. Momma won't allow that, I think. If I were to allow her to be out there that much, how would I have my clothing pressed and cleaned and dinner on the table? Not to mention, who would be watching over Momma when she isn't around to care for her? Momma is confined, you know. The news of.... Well, she never leaves her bed but to use the facilities and such. She'll need to care for her."

The man backed away when Brooke growled low. With a shake of his head, Danny told her that she could do whatever she wanted. Thomas reached for Brooke to show that she was his, and to tell the big man she was his to tell what she could and could not do, when he found himself on his back looking up at the blue cloudless sky. And his head hurt, terribly.

"Brooke, honey? I think I've fallen." Another growl, but this one was deeper, the sound of it very close to his face. Thomas looked at the weight he only just noticed on his chest, and saw the biggest dog he'd ever seen before. Then he realized it was a wolf. "Brooke? I need you to get a gun. Hurry now, before this thing decides to hurt me. Run along now, but don't try and fire it…that's not a woman's job but a man's, Momma told me."

"A man's job? Your momma needs to learn to keep her mouth shut, or someone is gonna teach her a few lessons in life. And I'm not going to do any such thing about getting you a gun. You're not going to shoot him, and I most certainly won't either. I like him a lot better than I do you." Thomas asked her how she knew a wolf. "I know all sorts of animals. I know a few Bengal tigers, some bears, as well as a few foxes and coyotes. We speak to each other a lot when I'm here. Alone. And I'm betting that any one of them would gladly eat you for dinner and no one would even care."

Thomas looked at Dick, who was nodding his head hard. Surely he couldn't be going along with her. She was off her noodle if she really believed she knew animals. And spoke to them as well. Thomas had been telling the people in town for years now that they needed to kill off all the animals in the valley and mountain. Now one of them had bitten his intended, and she was out of her head with some sort of mind melting sickness. His momma surely wouldn't be blaming this on him, would she? That was it, her mind had a fever and it wasn't his fault.

"You've been bitten by something, haven't you? Oh my, we're going to have to get you some help. I think it's done went and effected your thinking." The man, Doug, knelt down to him when the wolf growled again. "You have to get her to calm down so we can get her some help. I think...well, it's a good thing I'm still willing to marry her, what with her being insane and all, but she needs to get some help. My momma will be disappointed; you can bet she will. But then, everything disappoints her. Me too. But you'll help me, won't you, Doug?"

"Darcy. My name is Darcy Harrison. And the only help I'm going to be giving is to help you into your piece of shit truck and let you live another day." Thomas wasn't sure where all this meanness was coming from, and asked him about it. "Brooke is not going to marry you. She is not going to be taking care of your momma, who I think is a little on the sadistic side. Nor is she going to stop doing something that she loves very much. Now, what I'm also going to do for you is have the wolf here bite you. That way if you get it in your head again to kill even a mouse in these parts, he can and will hunt you down and kill you."

Thomas wasn't so sure about this biting thing. That just didn't set well with him. But before he could so much as make a comment on it, the sucker just nipped at his skin. He was pretty sure that the thing grinned at him. Then it occurred to him what Danny was saying.

"Kill me? For what?" Dillon stood up and laughed. The wolf moved off his chest and Thomas had to stay where he was for several minutes before he sat up. Brooke had left him there, without even letting him set up a time for them to go ring hunting. "Tell her that she needs help. I'm sure that you've been around her enough to know that she's not like this. Not normally so mean to people."

"I think that's all on you." Thomas was helped up, not gently either. When he'd taken Derek's hand he assumed it would be just a little lift. But he darn near threw him across the driveway. "Now, you get in that truck of yours and go away. I don't care where you go so long as it's not here. And don't show up again. Because her anger is not even going to be a drop of water compared to me getting pissed with you."

He grew. Thomas backed away from Dean when he seemed to just get bigger. Reaching for his door handle then remembering at the last minute that it had broken off yesterday, he reached into the truck to open his door. Before he could touch the handle, he was pressed hard against the door and told not to move.

"It's the only way I can get in." His hand was pulled free of his door and Dalton asked him if he had a gun. "Yes. What with all the animals about, everyone around here carries a gun. For protection. But it's not on the seat if you wanna borrow it to kill that wolf. You have to reach way up under the seat, on the other side. But I have to tell you, it's only got the one bullet in it. Momma told me never to leave more than just the one in case I hurt myself."

"I don't want to kill the wolf, you idiot." Thomas looked at him. He had a slight feeling that he might be willing to kill him, however. "Get in the truck."

The words were slurred, like he was having a hard time controlling some great monster. Nodding, Thomas got in his truck and turned the key. When he jumped forward because he'd forgotten to engage the clutch, he was sure that Danny was going to kill him.

"Darcy. Say it. My name is Darcy Harrison. I want you to remember it in the event that you return." Thomas asked him why it was important. "Because when I chase you down and kill you, I want you to know exactly who it was that did it."

Thomas nodded and started his truck up and carefully left the property. Before he was down the long winding driveway, he saw at least a dozen wolves running alongside him off and on. When he reached the main road, he pulled over and got out. Leaning over, he puked up his breakfast. Good heavens. Something was wrong up there. And whatever it was, he needed to get to Brooke and save her. Perhaps that man was feeding her something. Drugs.

He turned and looked up the mountain and wondered who that Darcy person thought he was, treating him like that. Thomas was going to go to the police as soon as he got into town. Darcy was doing something to his intended and it needed to stop. Getting into his truck, feeling a lot better now, Thomas decided that he needed to talk to his momma too. She'd know what else he should be doing to save Brooke from herself.

~~~

Darcy heard the music before he got to the building. He had to smile. Listening to classical music wasn't what he would have expected of her. But he supposed there were a great many things he still had to learn about his mate. Opening the door carefully, he stepped into a world so foreign to him, he just stood there and looked around.

Shelves lined the walls all over this part of the building. Most of them were filled with pottery, green ware he knew it was called; pottery that had been formed and designed, but not bisque fired nor glazed. He knew just from the sheer amount of what was around him that Brooke had been building up her inventory for some time. There had to be over two hundred pieces in varying sizes and shapes.

Plastic covered shelves with wheels sat in the middle of the brightly lit room. He had no idea what might be under the heavy, dirty plastic, but figured if he didn't piss off Brooke again, she might tell him. As much as he wanted to peek, he resisted. Not having any idea what stage the work might be in, he didn't know if lifting the covering would harm anything.

In the next room there were three potter's wheels. There were also large partitioned off areas that held boxes of clay, and large buckets with lids on them marked with different chemical names. He walked to the first of the wheels, careful of where he stepped, as there were broken pieces of clay as well as dust everywhere. Par for the course, he knew. Clay was a form of dirt, after all. He noticed the difference on each of them right away.

"I don't like to clean my wheel every time I have another project I'd like to do." He turned and looked at Brooke. She'd pulled on a muddy apron that had seen better days. There were no cute sayings on it, like *kiss the cook,* nor did there seem to be any pockets. "What are you doing in here?"

"I came to let you know that Thomas is gone. But I think he'll be back. How long has he been coming around with the intentions of getting you to marry him? And I'm wondering if you've met this famed momma of his." She didn't answer him then, but walked to one of the plastic draped shelves and pulled the covering off. Darcy wasn't prepared for the beauty of the work there. "Christ, that's beautiful."

"Dragons. I have been toying with them for months now. Grandda wasn't into working with clay this way, but did encourage me to try to work with it any way that I wanted.

70

He said that experimenting is what makes you find your greatness. And he told me he was still looking for his. This is my fifth try at it. I think I might have it now." He asked her what had happened before. "The first time I put the dragon on the piece as a solid work. I should have known better. It exploded in the first firing."

The form of the dragon was still in the beginning stages, but he could see him there. Part of his large body wrapped around the cylinder and his claws, really only tubes of clay, were clinging to the shape as if he were hanging onto it. Looking at the other four pieces, all of them the same shape and size as the first, Darcy could see that they too were part of the whole. He'd bet when this piece was finished that it would wrap around the castle, which seemed to be what it was clinging to, and look almost lifelike.

"When you get this finished, how big will it be?" He touched his finger to the second piece, which was more complete than the one she seemed to be inspecting. This one had scales, each of them handmade he'd bet, and put on the body one at a time. He saw that one of the claws had also been formed, and the nails, sharp and vicious looking, dug deep into the piece it clung to. "This is a castle, isn't it?"

"Yes. And it will be about six-foot-tall, give or take how much shrinkage I get. It'll be another couple of months before it's ready to be put in the first firing. Then I'll have to glaze it. I know what it's supposed to look like, but I have to run a few more glaze tests to make sure that I get the colors the way I want." He helped her pull the plastic back over the shelf. "Why are you here really, Darcy? And I don't mean in my shed, but here on my mountain. Why would you come here when I told you that my life is just the way I want it?"

He wasn't going to lie to her, even if he could have. She

71

was his mate and he wanted her trust as much as he did for her to love him. So sitting down on the room's only chair, he watched her fill a bucket with water and stand at the wheel in the middle.

"I guess you could say I thought that if I came here, I could convince you to let me be a part of your life. You'd get used to me hanging around, sort of see that I could be useful, then let me into your heart." She snorted at him and he laughed. "Yeah, I can see that was a major mistake now. As you said, you have your life all set up just fine. But now...well, now I love it here as well. The quietness of the area, the way that you could more than likely not see a person, at least most of the time, for days on end, and not have to deal with people. The woods are spectacular, and I'd bet in the spring and fall they're bright with color that an artist would have a hard time copying. In the summer they would be filled with animals that roam here, yet so few would see. Even the air seems cleaner to me."

"Those reasons and many more are why I don't like to leave." She picked up a roundish ball of clay and began shaping it with her hands. "We have all we want here. I put in a garden in the spring that will supply us with fresh vegetables. Meat isn't hard to come by either if we want to hunt. But we rarely kill any of the animals here for food. There is a grocery store that we can drive to, and I find it to be less stressful for me. I'm always afraid someone will kill a friend of mine and serve it up to me."

He laughed. "And Thomas? What is his deal?" She didn't say anything but did look sad. "He really thinks you're going to marry him. And knowing you, there is more than likely no reason for him to think that other than what's in his own head. Am I right?"

"Thomas started coming around about a month before Grandda got sick. I wasn't sure what he wanted at first; I thought he was trying to get money or a piece of pottery from him." He asked if that happened a lot. "Not really, but sometimes someone would come up here and ask for something for a benefit or an auction, and he'd donate a piece. He loved this area and would do just about anything for it. Anyway, Thomas. He came around for a week, then another, and finally Grandda asked me what I was going to do about him. I had no idea, so he told me what he'd been doing…asking for my hand in marriage. And as you might have guessed, his momma thought it was a good idea, and that I'd be manageable. Whatever the hell that was supposed to mean."

"I bet that went over well." Darcy watched her work the clay into a ball with her hands. She smacked it around a bit more until it was in whatever shape she needed, then put it on the wheel. Getting her hands wet, she pressed her body down on the ball and smashed it down. "He doesn't listen well… Thomas, I mean. No matter how many times he's told you're not interested, he has a one track mind about you. It's like my name. I'm thinking he decided I wasn't important enough for him to get to know, so he didn't bother."

"No doubt he only knows mine because he gets told it many times a day by Momma. But he didn't want to marry me for reasons that you're thinking. Not for money, like I first thought too. He has some…or so he's told me." Darcy decided to have someone look into his life, just to be sure he wasn't trying to scam anyone. "And then after Grandda passed, he was here nearly every day. I was sort of glad to leave to go to Ohio, he'd become such a pain in the ass."

"He'll be back; you know that, right?" She said that she did. "I wanted to tell you something else. You're not going to like it, so you might want to stop what you're doing for a moment."

"You're not leaving." He told her he wasn't. "Yeah, figured that one out too. I talked to Morgan a little bit, then his mate. I don't know what to do about you and this thing between us. I won't change my life. I like what I am and how I got here."

"I know you don't believe me, Brooke, but I don't want you to change either. As I said before, I like it here as well, and would like to spend the rest of my life here, with you."

The clay was a flat disk on the wheel. He did notice then that she threw on small pieces of wood, batts they were called, and when she was finished with a piece, she only had to pull the batt off the wheel and set it aside to start anew.

Her fingers moved along the outer edge of the disk. In one hand she held a small sponge; the other just had water dripping from her fingertips. When she pinched her hand and the sponge together and lifted, the clay moved up, making at first a cone, then a tall cylinder. When it was perhaps seven or eight inches tall, she wet her sponge and fingers and widened the clay out. This made it look like a straight sided bowl now.

Picking up a small disk of wood, she slid it up the side of the bowl shape, smoothing out all the finger marks, and then she made a lip. In less than two minutes she'd made a beautiful bowl large enough to sit a small child in.

"You have the funniest look on your face." He looked at her when she spoke and wondered if she realized how incredibly beautiful she was. "Have you never seen someone throw before?"

"Yes. A long time ago. Your grandda I think it was, as a matter of fact. No one seemed to know his name even back then." She nodded, and he knew that the memory of him was painful for her. "This little older man was sitting outside a building on the strip, just talking a mile a minute to anyone that stood there, and making these small little pots. My mom and I got several of them for the little neighborhood girls who did tea parties with their dolls. We got little pitchers and cups. They were amazingly detailed and well done. I still have a set of them, I think."

"He called that his show stoppers. I remember watching him work the crowd, and wondered what he could possible say to so many people that had them coming back again and again. As you might have figured out, he didn't need you to talk back to him…he could talk your arm off and you not say a single word." Darcy got up and stood behind her. When she leaned into him, her back flush with his chest, he wrapped his arms around Brooke and held her. "I'm not going to be able to resist you much longer. I have a need for you to take me, anywhere. And it's making me insane trying not to think about sex with you."

"I want you to need me for more than just sex." She told him he did chop a mean cord of wood. "Good, I'd hate to be completely useless to you."

Turning Brooke in his arms, he kissed her. As much as he didn't want to rush them, he knew that it was well beyond their control now. Lifting her up, he groaned when she wrapped her legs around his waist, and Darcy carried her to the table behind them. Sitting her on it, he pulled her sweatshirt up and over her head.

"Christ."

She was bare to him. No bra, not even a tee shirt to hide the beauty that was in front of him. Lifting one of her heavy breasts up, he took it to his mouth and suckled hard. Brooke's fingers in his hair holding him to her had him pulling her to the edge of the table so that he could strip her naked. With

75

Brooke's help he had her pants off, as well as her too large boots.

When she was naked, spread out before him, Darcy pulled his own shirt off and dropped it on top of her clothing. He debated for all of a second on whether or not to strip down as well, but she took over. When his pants were undone, Brooke slipped her hand into his boxers and cupped his cock. He rocked into her palm like he wanted to her body, taking them both over the edge of sanity, several times before he would like, only to begin again.

"You're making it very hard to think of how I need to make love to you." Instead of speaking, she leaned in and kissed him. Pulling his pants down to his hips, he freed his cock and she fisted him. "Christ, you're killing me."

"I need to taste you." Darcy stepped back. While the thought of her mouth on his cock nearly made him come, he was too close, too needy to have her do that this time. He wasn't going to come in his mate for the first time in her mouth. But knowing that she was a virgin also gave him pause. He needed to take things very slowly this first time. "Darcy, I'm so close to coming that I could make myself come with just a touch of my finger."

"Do it. I want to watch you."

While she held him with one hand, she slid her other down her breasts to her navel. Darcy's mouth watered to follow the same path with his mouth, but he traced her movements with his fingers, touching her where she did.

Then when she moved over her navel, he leaned down and licked her small indentation with his tongue. Darcy feasted on her flesh, taking nips at her dewy skin, licking the small wounds he made so that she'd not be hurt. But he could smell her stronger now, this close to where he wanted to taste her.

When she spread her legs wider, her hand just above the hair there, he wrapped his hand around hers and slid her fingers in with his. Christ, she was wet and her clit as hard as he was.

Heat engulfed him. She soaked his hand with her cream and rode him like it was his cock. Darcy watched their fingers fuck her, sliding in and out of her as her hips moved back and forth. The thought of sliding into her, filling her up, made his cock leak more, to ache to be so close to paradise and not be able to touch. When she moved their hands and pulled his cock to her, he slid just his crown into her and held her as still as he could while he fucked her this way. He knew that he would hurt her when he took her, and hated to think about causing her pain, any kind of pain.

"I need to come." Darcy leaned into her throat, licking the pulse there while she held onto him. "Darcy, please. I'm so close, I need it. Please."

He bit down on her throat as he filled her. When she screamed, her body tightening around his, he stilled his own movements, trying not to take her as hard as he wanted. Darcy held her tightly to him and tried to think past the love that just poured over him for this woman.

Brooke was his. And Darcy was never going to leave her... only by death could he. Which might be sooner than he'd hope if he didn't come soon, he thought.

CHAPTER 5

It was too much and not nearly enough. His cock seemed to vibrate within her. Brooke wanted to beg him to leave her alone, but she also knew that if he did, she'd never reach whatever pinnacle was right there. Moving her hips just enough to try and get into a more comfortable position, she moaned when he grabbed her hips and told her to be still.

"You move and I'll come inside of you right now." That didn't sound like a bad plan and she told him that. "But if I come in you this way and not the way that I want, you're going to be disappointed in me."

"I doubt that. Just give me a little." He moved his hips and she cried out again. Not in pain, but the most incredible pleasure she'd ever experienced. But still, it wasn't nearly what she knew was coming "Oh Darcy, again. Please, that was so good, move again."

He did so, moving his hips enough that she could feel his cock moving deeper inside of her, filling her tightly. So much so that she was sure she could feel every vein, every muscle, along his shaft. Holding onto his shoulders, she lifted her hips up when he stroked her, and knew that this was what it was supposed to feel like...this was going to bring her such pleasure. Each time he lifted her up with his hand on her ass, it felt as if he brought her closer to the edge of something extraordinary. And every time his groin touched her, he was giving her more than she ever dreamed possible in sex.

"Lean back for me, Brooke. I need to taste more of you." She did as he asked, watching his cock as it filled her over and over. Her juices were making him slick, and she knew that her body had made him this hard, this needy. "Christ, you're so tight, so wet. My cock is aching to come."

"Yes. I want to feel it...come for me so that you can bring me, Darcy. Please, come for me."

He leaned over then, pressing her back into the table, and took her breast in his mouth. As he devoured her, Brooke lifted it up and fed him. He was taking her harder now, his cock moving faster and faster. When he bit her again, suckled hard on the wound she knew that he'd given her, Brooke felt her entire being freeze, her heart stopped beating, breath was impossible to take. Then she exploded. There was no other name for what happened...Brooke's body exploded.

Screaming out the pleasure of the climax took her breath away again. Even as he continued to pound into her, his mouth and hands touching her, she felt her body turn inside out and tighten again. When he lifted her up, pulled her body to his, she cried out when her back touched the wall. He fucked her so hard then that she felt the wall behind her shake with it.

"Come." She cried out when her body did as he wanted. And it was her body that came, all of her, and not just her pussy. When he tilted his head, offering her his throat, Brooke saw the pulse there, his vein throbbing with his blood, and her mouth watered to taste him. She needed to do as he'd done to her and bite him. Leaning to him, her mouth right over the flesh that she could almost taste, he begged her to bite him, to drink from him. Brooke sank her teeth into him as her body came apart again when he did, his body bowing back as he filled her.

His blood tasted coppery, but sweet too. Swallowing it past her throat, she cried out again and again as she came. Each time her body flew apart, Darcy seemed to be right there to put her back together again, only to take her once more. When she lifted her head from his throat, she saw him then, the cat that had eaten her earlier, as it seemed to race over his skin showing her that he was there for her forever. And as she watched the big cat, Brooke knew that she would forever belong to them both.

He fucked her through three more powerful climaxes until she begged him to let her rest. Brooke held onto him as he moved them to the chair, never letting him go with her body or legs that still were wrapped around him. Thinking that he'd sit her down and get dressed, she was surprised when he sat her on his lap and held onto her hips. She moved to stand and felt his cock jerk in her pussy.

"I'd really love for you to ride me this way." That sounded wonderful, but she wasn't sure how to accomplish that and told him. Darcy put his hands on her hips and showed her, rolling her forward and back much like one would ride the back of a horse. But this was oh so much better. "If you come on me this way, I can watch every part of you as you do."

Each time her clit touched his groin, she felt it everywhere. It made her want to go faster, touch him more and harder. It was like he was using her vibrator on her; the sensation was so amazing that she wanted it all. When he lifted her breasts up, cupping them in his hands, she felt her juices gush as he fed from first one, then the other. Rolling her hips faster, she held onto him as he looked up at her.

"I'm going to bite you here. Would you like that?" She couldn't answer him verbally but nodded her consent; her mouth had suddenly gone dry. When he leaned in and nipped at her breast, she came hard, a quick punch to her system that made her beg him for more. "Come for me, Brooke. Come while I drink from you."

When he bit down on her again, Brooke knew that she was going to black out. And when he pinched her clit with his free hand, she felt the darkness simply swallow her up. Christ, the man had killed her.

When she woke up she was in her bed. The shower was running in her bathroom, so she knew that Darcy was still close. Pulling the covers up to her chin, she started to panic just a little when she thought of what he was going to do to her now.

You're all right. I'm here. His voice was soft in her head, and she felt her nerves start to soothe. *I had to shower some of your clay off me before I joined you in the bed. You sort of smeared it all over my back and arms.*

We had sex. He told her that he'd loved every minute of it. *I mean, we're not going to be able to part now if you should need to.*

I can see no reason that I'd ever want to part from you. I might have to go up to Ohio a few times a year. I have projects going there that I can't leave unfinished. And there is my family. Who wants you to come and visit when you want, by the way. He didn't tell her she was going, nor did he say that they were going to move to his home state. *Brooke, I'm not going to make you do anything you don't want to. I'm just as happy to be here as I have been anywhere in my life.*

There are times when I can't leave for weeks on end. I have orders stacking up now that make me a little anxious about getting them done. My clay is brought to me, supplies too. I have someone come in and help with the housework a few times a month and buy food, but I don't go into town on a whim. I don't do parties or go to movies. I'm here because I like it here.

He came out of the bathroom and stood there with a towel around his waist. When he sat down on the edge of the bed, she felt her panic start to take over again.

The kiss was unexpected, though not unwelcomed by any means. It calmed her, made her forget what she was upset about. And when he laid down beside her on the bed, she realized she was naked and felt her body heat up. When he curled his big body around hers, spooning against her, she felt warm, relaxed, and a feeling that she had no name for just now.

"You should know that while I do enjoy an occasional movie, I'm not nuts about going to a theater to see them. Too many people who can't keep their mouths shut or put their cell phones away enough to enjoy what is in front of them. Dinner? Okay, I do go out to eat a lot. But only because it's too much effort to go and buy food, bring it home, and cook it for just one person. Then there is the whole cleaning up thing. Not how I want to spend my time." She asked him if he could cook. "I can, as a matter of fact. All of my brothers can. Mom made sure that we could so we'd know our way around a kitchen. None of my married brothers cook, nor do their wives, but that's fine with them too. I actually like cooking."

"I don't care for it at all. I mean, I can fix a sandwich or pancakes, bake a potato if I want one, but I'd just as soon not have to bother. Usually my mind is on some project, and I forget to eat until I'm dizzy." He told her that he'd cook for them if that was all right. "If you want. What else are you going to do all day? I'm not able to change my work schedule around to suit you."

"And I don't expect you to. I noticed that you have a computer, so I'm assuming that you have Internet." She said that she did. "Well, I can work from here until I need to go in person. Most of my work with the family firm is done in the office anyway, so the only difference now is my scenery. I didn't snoop around except to find your room when I came in the house, but I'm hoping there is a place for me to set up an office. If you don't mind."

She wanted to ask him how long he would be okay with this. When did he think he was going to grow bored with the way she lived her life here and leave her for good? But he kissed her on the shoulder then, and she felt tears fill her eyes and her heart hurt. Brooke had only just realized that she really liked this man, and was going to truly miss him if he left her.

"I was wondering something." She said nothing as he continued. "When I was chopping wood this morning, I couldn't help but notice that there is a lot of wood stacked up to use. Not just where I was working, but at different points on the property. I can understand that chopping it where it is makes sense, but no matter how you chop it, it's still a lot of wood. Do you heat this house with it or use it in the pottery?"

"There's a hot oven—my grandda and I built it—in the kitchen, one that makes really good baked bread and pizza, and uses wood to fire up. The house is heated by natural gas that belongs to us. There are a couple of kilns that use electric, but I don't use those much. I like firing in the outdoors using gas or wood when I can. But the bulk of the wood is for the once a year firing that we do in the mountain. It also helps clear away the dead logs that seem to gather late in the fall, and keeps the property well maintained. The firing of the mountain kiln happens in the late winter, or sometimes the early spring. Even for being outside, it gets fucking hot out there. In fact, we're going to be using it in two weeks, the week after Christmas."

"I read up on that before Mac and I drove down here. It's

supposed to be like this huge party, right?" She rolled to her back and looked up at him. "What is it, love?"

"I should have canceled it. I wanted to, but Grandda told me that life was to go on after he passed. Said that people depended on the firing for their livelihood, and if I canceled it because he had to go on to see his Maker, then that would be unfair to them." He kissed her gently but didn't say anything. "When he got really sick and with that weaker, he told me that I had to do my best to keep making it so others could see his mountain work. Not just his pottery, but mine as well. He considered me to be his work."

"He sounded like an amazing man. I doubt that anyone who knew him would have thought he was this famous artist that, like you, had his pieces all over the world. He just looked like this grizzly of a man who liked people and playing with clay." Brooke smiled at the description of her favorite person in the world. "You're a great deal like him, I think. Not the man nor the grizzly part, but I mean good with people. I watched you at the gallery. You did well for someone who doesn't care for people."

"He made me feel safe and to believe in myself. He was very good at seeing the potential in people and helping them to bring it out." Darcy kissed her again and she felt her body respond to it. When he moved down her body, kissing her throat, nibbling on her earlobe, and then to her breast, she reached down and wrapped her hand around his cock. "I love the way that you make me feel when you touch me. Your hands are strong and callused, and I can feel each little hard place when you touch me."

He dipped his tongue into her belly button and she moaned. "I have been wanting to do that for days now. Taste you here. Christ, do you have any idea how lovely you are?"

"Pretty, I guess, but not lovely." He pinched her hip and she squealed. "What was that for? That hurt."

"You're beautiful, and mine." His mouth was over her pussy, and she felt it heat in anticipation of his tongue touching her; wetness spread under her bottom and her breath caught. When he kissed her just above her hairline, she closed her eyes and waited for him to take her. "Watch me, Brooke. I want you to see how much I enjoy feasting on you."

His kiss on her pussy gave her a hot short climax. When he flicked his tongue into her nether lips, she moaned and begged him for more. Just as she was ready to pull him to her, have him eat her as he'd promised, the big tiger was there, his eyes as green as Darcy's had been.

With the tiger lapping at her, she spread her legs wider for him. The cat's big head was larger than Darcy's, his tongue longer and thicker. But it was the roughness of it that brought her so much pleasure, and every time he licked her, she knew he was teasing her. Nothing could have prepared her for the sensation of his tongue entering her and touching off a climax that had her screaming at the top of her lungs.

More. Give him more. She wasn't sure she had anything left in her when Darcy commanded her to come again. But as soon as the cat's tongue fucked her again and again, Brooke screamed out a second then a third climax before she put her hand on his head and pulled him away.

"You have to stop." The cat licked her again, making her shudder, her body feeling like it had been shocked with a live wire. His tongue touched off another release, and finally she had to beg him to move. But before she could get up, Darcy was there, his mouth poised over her. "Fuck me."

"I need a taste of you too." She cried out when he took her clit into his mouth and bit down. *You taste of honey, sweet honey.*

86

He ate her like he was a starved man. Every time she came, each time she begged him to stop, he would take her again, bringing her over the edge so many times she was weak with it. But when he moved up her body, his cock thick and dark purple with need, she rolled him to his back and told him it was her turn.

~~~

Darcy held his cock for her when she moved down his body. He hurt, he needed to come so badly. When she licked him from root to tip, it was all he could do not to come all over her. And when she took him into her mouth, he had to grip the bed and count to ten so that he wouldn't roll her over and fuck her.

"Do you hurt?" He told her that he did, badly. "If you came, would you feel better? I know that when I come all over your cock, I feel fantastic."

"You're not helping." It was in that moment, when she giggled, that he realized what she was doing...teasing him. "Christ, woman, you're going to kill me. Just let me fuck you and we'll both feel better."

"But I want you to come down my throat. I need that." He groaned, then cried out when she cupped his balls in her hand. "So warm. Can I taste them as well?"

He might have answered her, he wasn't sure. But as soon as she sucked one than the other into her mouth, he felt his cock jerk painfully. Wrapping his hand into her hair, Darcy tried to pull her off him, but she dug her nails into his hips and he begged her to finish him.

"Not yet."

Brooke nipped at his shaft, following the vein from tip to groin with her very talented tongue. When she sucked on him, Darcy fucked her pretty mouth hard, still begging her to let him come. And when she started fisting him, her hand using both her saliva and his precum to make the slide faster, he rose up with each of her downward strokes until he felt his climax take him.

His cum hit her in the face, mouth, and chin. She didn't stop fisting him as he wrapped his hand around hers, showing her how to help him as he sprayed her over and over. When she sat up on her knees, her body glistening with his cum, Darcy grabbed her and tossed her to her belly and got up behind her.

Slamming his cock into her pussy, he fucked her hard, taking her to the bed as he leaned down and bit her over and over. Each time she cried out, screamed his name, he'd bite her again, all the while his cock never stopped. The need to dominate, to show her he was hers, made him reckless in his taking her, completely forgetting that she may be sore. And when she begged him for more, he reached under her, touched her clit with his thumb and fingers and pinched.

Darcy came when she did, her body so tight around his that he felt strangled, like his cock had been put into a vise and squeezed...but in the most pleasurable way imaginable. Coming in her this way, fucking her like his animal would, he came twice more. When he threw back his head and roared out, Darcy felt everything around him simply snap out.

When he woke the room was dark. He sat up knowing that he was alone, not just in the room but the house as well. Reaching out to Brooke, he found her in the shed working, her mind and body completely focused on what she was doing. Getting up, going into the bathroom, he was just washing up his hair when he felt the familiar touch of his dad. Smiling, he asked him how he was.

Fine. Right as rain, as a matter of fact. I was wondering something. I found...well, Nikki and I found something in an old paper that you might be able to answer for me. Oh, I'm to tell you that your mother is disappointed in you that you've not called her once since you got yourself a mate. There was no censure there, just his dad giving him a hard time. *There was this mention of an unsolved murder of sorts. It claims that maybe a man by the name of Rickson was in some trouble about murdering someone, but there seemed not to be enough evidence to make anything stick. Will Graceson was involved in some kind of hit and run. This guy's name is...let me look here. Blake Rickson. That's the name of her uncle, isn't it?*

Yes, and Brooklynn was Brooke's mom and William — I think he went by Will — was her father. I don't know anything about that, Dad. What does it say? I mean, Brooke talked about her mom passing away a few days after Brody was born, brokenhearted she said. Do you think that Blake killed her dad and that was what killed her mom? Other than the small amount that she's told me I know very little, and it never occurred to me that she might think he did it. Her dad was killed in a hit and run when a robbery went wrong, right? His dad said that the paper didn't come out and say it, but heavily implied it. *How would I go about figuring this out? I mean, if Blake is responsible for maybe one or even two murders, there is no telling what he'll do to Brooke to get what he wants.*

That's the route we were going. He was quiet for a moment. *I have an idea. I don't know if you're going to like it much, but I'm gonna throw it out there. This mountain that she lives on, are there any hotels or such around? Perhaps big enough to hold all of us for the holidays?*

You mean all of you coming down here to help me watch her under the pretense of Christmas? Dad, you're as transparent as ever. But she's not even put up a tree or anything. I'm not sure what she is planning. All I can tell you is that I'll talk to her about it. He asked him if he'd do that for him. *What if she says she can't do it... celebrate with all of us? I won't force her to.*

Well of course you won't. Just ask her, and if she says no then we'll think of something else. But to my way of thinking, this Blake person, he's not going to let this money go without some sort of payback to her. And with you being right there, he's gonna feel like you're peeing in his pot. Oh, and you might want to let Brooke know that her Brody is staying with Storm and Riordan. She picked him up one day when she saw that he was in a bit of trouble. Nice kid, that boy. Darcy said he'd tell her and was pretty sure Dad was right about Blake. *You talk to her. We'll make some kind of arrangements on our end, even if it's only to go there and see you on Christmas Day and come on back. I need my kids around me, you know that.*

Darcy knew that. Christmas was his dad's favorite time of the year. He thought he loved it more than Mom did, and she really went all out. Going to the kitchen, thinking about all the things he needed to do before he went back up to Ohio to get his things, he wondered what Brooke did for the holidays. Perhaps he could even make it look like they were bringing his things to him and decided to celebrate too. Nah, he thought, he wasn't going to do that. It was a good plan, but seemed underhanded somehow.

When he had everything ready, just needing to pop biscuits in the oven and cook the eggs, he reached out to Brooke and asked her if she was hungry. Her laughter made him think she'd forgotten about food.

Yes, I can eat. I think there is some cereal in the cabinets if you want to share that with me. I don't have a lot of time right now to fix something more if you want it. He asked her how she liked her eggs. *Poached. But you don't have to make that. I'll just eat something cold for now.*

It's done. Just clean up if you can, and by the time you get in here, things will be ready. And as soon as you're done eating, you can go back to work. I have things under control here. She seemed a

90

little hesitant. *If you don't have time to come in now, that's all right. I know how it is when you're in the middle of something important. Anything that I have ready can be saved and eaten later. Really, honey, it's not that big of a deal.*

I'm coming in. He asked her if she was all right with that. *Yes, more than all right. But you don't have to wait on me. I'm perfectly fine with eating whatever is in the cabinets.*

Yes, I'm sure you are, and maybe there will be times when we eat that, but I'm hungry. I worked up a hell of an appetite last night, thanks to you. Besides, I wanted to try out your kitchen. Sometime when you have a few minutes, maybe you can show me how to use this oven. Christ, I can almost taste pizza coming out of it.

When she laughed, he put the biscuits in the hot oven and set the timer. By the time she came in the house, not only were the biscuits golden brown, but he had three poached eggs done and the table set. Darcy was pretty sure he could get used to this.

CHAPTER 6

"She's shacked up with that guy who had me arrested. The one I was telling you about." Blake knew that. He'd been keeping tabs on Brooke since Benson had called to tell him he needed bail money. "Do you think he's there to get her money? If he is, the fucker is gonna be sadly disappointed. She's tighter with that money than Grandda was. And he made spending any of it seem like a fucking crime."

"No, I told you, the money can't go to anyone but her. She can hand it out, like she should be to us, but no one can inherit it, nor can they profit off it unless they marry her. And we both know she's never going to do that. No man alive would put up with her shit." No, Brooke didn't trust anyone, and hated men with a passion. He'd made sure of that every day of her life when she'd been stupid enough to get around him when they were alone. "I still can't believe my own grandfather did this to me. His only grandchild and he leaves me out in the cold. I'm telling you right now, if I had the money to sue her, I'd do it. She's not being fair with this shit."

Grandda had really left him high and dry, and as broke as he could be. No special pieces of Grandda's work had been left to him—not that Blake thought any of it was all that special, but he could have given him at least a couple of pieces so he could make some cash. But there wasn't mention of him getting

93

anything in the will, only that he'd already received his money in the form of bail, payoffs, and theft. He'd not even left him a lousy five bucks to buy a cup of coffee. How fucking selfish could one man be, for Christ's sake? And to leave Benson out of it too? Fuck that stuff. Blake had hoped that one of them would be all right, and if it might have been Benson.... Well, he'd be taking it from him a hell of a lot easier than he was from his niece. And where the fuck was Brody in all this? He could usually be good to knock around for a couple hundred.

Blake had figured all along that he'd be ripped off when his grandfather died. But his plan had been to cultivate his nephew into giving him a large part of whatever he got. The kids, all that was left of Grandda's dear Brooklynn, were sure to get one third of the vast estate that was Rickson. But he'd fucked him over even in that.

"Tell me again why we can't sell the story off that she's this famous person. I mean, I bet there are all kinds of tabloids just waiting to give us something for that piece of information." He knew that there were too. But he couldn't do it. Not because of it being his niece, but if he did it, then there would be a hundred more reasons he'd never get what he wanted. He'd signed a nondisclosure form before the will had been read, and if he even hinted at what he knew, then prison would be the least of his worries. Grandda had said that Morgan and his pack would take care that he never collected a penny off the story should he do that.

"What do you think will happen if the world knows that on that mountain is one of the richest women in the world? Huh? Do you suppose they'll sit by and wait for her to come into town to get a gallon of milk before they try and get a piece of her? No. They'll be all over her, crawling into her bed, claiming her for their own, and trying their best to get our money. And you know as well as I do that even if we were to do it — and I'm not saying that I will, but you signed that form too — we'd both be as dead as that old man. And I'm betting that Morgan would kill us right out in the open and not give two shits if he had witnesses or not." The way the town was treating him right now, he was pretty sure they might hold him down while Morgan tore his throat out, too. Blake wasn't well liked, neither was Benson. And going to the papers was what had gotten him into trouble with his grandfather in the first place. "Men will try to kidnap her, hold her for ransom, and then what will we do? Nothing. Because as surely as we're standing here, we both know that as soon as she opens her mouth to one of them, they're gonna kill her. She's not a nice person when pressed. Then all the money goes to the charity that Grandda set up in the event that she died before he did. What a fucked up way to not give us what we deserve."

"Yeah, I forgot about that." He was forever forgetting all kinds of shit of late. Blake was pretty sure that Benson was using again, and he knew that he was sick…more than likely dying. Where he was getting the money for drugs was beyond him, but so long as he didn't hit him up for any, then they were just fine. "I tried again to get to the shed. She's got more locks and cameras on that thing than the bank downtown has. It's like she doesn't trust any of us."

"And with good reason." Blake had been to the shed too. Not only was there more security on it, like Benson said, but the pack roamed the woods and surrounding area like they were getting paid for it. He wondered briefly if they were and dismissed it. Morgan loved Brooke and thought of her as pack. He'd be doing her a favor by keeping him out. Fucker. The pack needed to be killed, and he was going to do it as soon as he had all the money.

"She's not canceled that big party thing like you said she would. In fact, one of my buddies heard tell that she was bringing in a side of beef to be roasted for them artist types. And having all kinds of tents and shit put up for it. Christ, what a waste of good food and money. She should be giving that to us, not trying to be like Grandda, who she will never be like." Benson made it sound as if being an artist was a profession lower than anything. But as far as Blake could see, Brooke had surpassed Grandda and his artistic abilities a long time ago. She was fucking awesome at it. But he'd never say that to her. Blake supposed to Benson it might well be a waste of money to do all this. However, if they were there, perhaps it would be a good opportunity to get into the house to grab some of the shit that was just waiting to be pawned for cash. Blake just stared at Benson when he seemed to be reading his thoughts. "Do you think we can blend in? Get some food then hit her?"

"I'm thinking that if we don't have something from her by this firing party, then we have to do something drastic. I'm not above kidnapping Brooke and holding her until she tells someone to pay us off. And she'll keep paying us too." Benson nodded. "It would be nice if we could get into the house and take a few pieces of Grandda's work. It's not like she'd miss any of them. Christ, when I lived there, you couldn't take a dump without seeing a dozen or so in the bathroom with you. Something like that would go a long way to keeping us in money. I'm sick to death of being broke all the fucking time."

"I'm working on that. Like I said, she's got that place all wired up like she doesn't want anyone in either the shed or the house." Blake didn't point out that was the reason, but let Benson go on. "I know where all the pieces are in the house. You know that she hasn't touched any except to dust them off. I was thinking about getting in there and just taking what I can carry out. I can take some kind of carrying thing to bring them down. My car just won't make those mountains anymore. Not too much going on around the house so long as she's not in it."

"You mean the pack doesn't watch the house unless she's in it? Why didn't you tell me this before?" He said that he had, but Blake would have remembered that. "You need to get in there and bring out those pieces, and I'll help you bring them down. If we work together, we can get a lot more than just a couple of them, don't you think? Maybe enough to live on or get an attorney or something. I have to pay some on my rent or I'm out on my ass in a couple of weeks. I'll set it up with someone I know that can hock it for us."

By the time Benson left to go and hide out until he could get into the house, Blake had made some calls. Two to some fencers that he knew, and one to his guy, Fletcher Crocker, Fletch to his friends. He'd been watching over Brody since he left the hospital in Ohio...or had been trying to keep up with Brody. The kid could get away from his tags faster and better than anyone he'd ever known. And Blake would bet his last dollar that Brody wasn't even aware that he was being followed. The shit was costing Blake money all the time too. But Fletch was willing to wait on some cash until after he was able to knock some sense into either Brody or Brooke. One of them was going to pay up. But Fletch had no good news.

"I can't find him. Christ, it's like he's a fucking ghost. Didn't I tell you the last time you set me on him that he has this sixth sense about shit?" He had, but Blake still wanted Fletch watching out for him. "I had it in my head when this thing started with watching this kid that it would be a piece of cake. He's afflicted...how hard can it be to keep an eye on him? But Christ, one minute he can be waiting on a bus to pick him up, and I swear to you, it's like he disappears. I had him dead to rights just a couple of days ago, when this broad shows up and sits at the table with him. Next thing I know, not only is his place cleaned out, but there's not a trace of him anywhere. Not even at his old haunts."

"What broad?" Fletch described her as tall, butch, and sort of mouthy. "You got the mouthy part because she saw you? Or you heard her talking to Brody that way?"

"She saw me but didn't know me. I bumped into her and came away feeling like I'd been beaten to fuck by a ball bat. Threw me to the ground and had her gun at my head in a heartbeat. I tried to tell her it was an accident, which to be honest it was, but she wasn't having it. Brody didn't know me, if that's what you're gonna say next." Brody had better not know Fletch. It was what kept the man alive. "When she finally let me up, with a warning of all things, I got out of there as quick as I could. Brody has been a ghost since."

He'd been trying for the last two months, since Grandda had died, to get Brody. He'd almost had him twice now, once at the funeral then a couple of days later. His plan had been to hold Brody until Brooke paid him. Benson didn't know about that plan, and wasn't going to if Blake could swing it. But it was looking to be as bad a bust as the one of them getting into the shed to get some of the older pieces to sell off. What the hell did she need all that pottery for anyway? It wasn't like she had that many shelves for it.

After hanging up with Fletch, he decided to see if he could talk to Brooke again. The phone number that he had to the house was private, and it had cost him all the money he'd had to get it, but he was going to talk to her and by God she was going to listen to him. He was her oldest living relative and it was time she started showing him some respect. Smiling to himself, he called the house. When a man answered it, his voice sounding slightly annoyed, Blake hung up and tried again, sure he'd put in the wrong number.

"Hello, this is the Rickson residence." Nope, right house, so he'd not dialed the wrong number. He waited for the man to say more, like who the fuck he was, but when he laughed, Blake felt his balls tighten to his body. "Is this Blake or Benson? Either one of you are fucking with the wrong family if that's who is calling and trying to act all stealthy by not talking. Won't work by the way, I got your number."

"Where's Brooke? Tell her it's her uncle and I want to talk to her." The man laughed again. "Are you cruising for a bruising, buddy? I'm in no mood for you to be fucking around. Get Brooke on the phone right now, and when I see you, I'll let you off with only an ass stomping."

"How kind of you. Only an ass stomping, huh? Well, I hate to break it to you, Blake my boy, but I don't think you have it in you to take me on. And as much as I'd love to take you down, I can't. Not yet at any rate. But you keep fucking around and I won't have a problem with it." Blake thought of the man that Benson had described to him, and figured maybe he was pulling his leg just a little. "Why don't you come on up here and let me show you how we treat people who threaten our mates? Yes, so you don't have to overtax your tiny brain, Brooke is my mate."

It hit him then. Mates, they were mates. Which meant that this guy could easily kill him, and would if he fucked around with Brooke. But only if he was to get caught. And Blake had learned that not getting caught was easier than people believed it to be. He'd been killing for years and no one even looked his way.

"You're not human." The man laughed and said he was right. "One of those fucking pack dogs, I bet. Nothing but a mongrel that shits in the same place it eats. You should know that I don't scare easily, and dogs for the most part are too stupid to do anything but breed. Is that what you are? A fucking mutt?"

"No, not a mutt. I'm a tiger, a Bengal. The whole Harrison family is…purebloods too, if you want the entire truth. And big fuckers, in the event you want to cause us any trouble." Blake sat down. Regular tigers were fucking huge, and if this man wasn't lying to him, then he was going to be bigger. Meaner too, if Blake was caught trying to hurt Brooke. "Are you rethinking this whole stupid plan of yours to make Brooke's life harder than it is? I have to tell you, Blake, I'm hoping you aren't. Rethinking this stupid plan of yours. Because it would make me feel really good to take care of you for her."

"Are you threatening me, Harrison? I surely hope not. I don't know how things are done in your neck of the woods, but we don't take kindly to someone threatening us like that. Especially family…and we are family now, aren't we?" Harrison assured him that he wasn't threatening him at all. "Well that's good. But you should also remember that blood is thicker than water, and I'm pretty sure that we both know who would come out on top if Brooke had to choose."

"First of all, I want to clear a few things up with you. I wasn't threatening you, Blake, but telling you for a fact that if you come here with intent to harm her, there won't be any part of your body ever found. I will even put that in writing for you should you want it. Also—and this is something I doubt very much you've thought through—yes, blood is thicker than water, but she doesn't like you much, so I'm thinking I'll be on top if it came down to it." Harrison's voice got hard then and carried the promise through the phone very well. Well enough, in fact, to make Blake feel like his bladder wasn't going to hold water. "If I find you or Benson anywhere near the shed, Brooke, or this house again, I will help those pack dogs, as you called them, find you and end your fucking miserable life."

The line went dead. Not so much as if Harrison had just hung up, but it was as if he'd cut the line. Blake put the handset in the cradle and stared at it. He had not just been told he was going to fucking be killed by this man, but he thought for sure that he'd enjoy it as well. Blake decided that from now on, Benson would be the one who did whatever it took to get the money from Brooke. Blake wasn't going anywhere near the mountain again until this shit was over. Not even to go in and get what he felt should have been rightfully his in the first place.

~~~

Storm could tell that Brooke wasn't thrilled about them being there. Not that she blamed her much. It was a lot to take in having this family, all of them, under one roof. She wondered what she'd say if she found out that some of the gifts that were being delivered in the morning were from the president, and one of them was a lovely wedding present. She'd more than likely go out to her building, never to return.

When she looked at the door for the fifth time in as many minutes, Storm decided to help her out. Standing up, she made her way to the beautiful woman and wasn't surprised to see her backing up. She got that a lot, but it didn't make her feel any better to have someone in her family do it.

"You know that I won't hurt you, don't you?" Brooke nodded, then shook her head. "Just what did Darcy tell you about me? I'm assuming it wasn't all good."

"Oh no. It was nice. He just said that you carried a gun and weren't afraid to use it if you needed to. I'm just trying to figure out the boundaries that you have to not use it on me.

101

Plus, having you all here, it's a lot when you've lived alone for as long as I have. Not to mention, they're all fucking big, aren't they?" When she grinned at her, Storm decided that she liked this woman. "Just so you know, I can get rid of a body too if need be. And I think much better, too. Kilns make the perfect disposal system. Even guns and knives can be dealt with nicely if it comes to that."

"I see. And how many times have you used this method of ridding yourself of bodies?" Brooke pretended to think it over, then smiled at her and told her not often enough. "Blake and Benson, I'm guessing, would be high on that list of bodies to get rid of if necessary."

"Yes. Did Darcy tell you that he talked with my uncle before you got here?" He had, but Storm asked her what he'd said. "I don't think Blake said much of anything. Darcy, however, had plenty to say. I had no idea...well, I mean I guess I could have guessed that under that calmness there lurked a monster waiting to get out. I think even Darcy was a little surprised at how easy it was to threaten and mean every word of it. He told Blake that if he came here to try and hurt me, he'd kill him."

"Good for you both." Brooke said nothing, but Storm had a feeling that she still wasn't sure about this. "He won't hurt you."

"Oh, I know. But my uncle and brother will. I'm not so stupid as to think that Darcy can protect me all the time. There are limits to everyone's ability to do that. Even you." Storm nodded. "I don't carry a gun, but I have other means of dealing with Blake if he tries anything. There is an entire pack here that I can call on."

"The Boyer Pack." Brooke didn't even seem surprised that she knew of them. "There are others here too. Men that I put in place when Darcy moved here to be with you."

"I know that too. One is living for the most part in the barn. He needs to go further from his hiding place to pee if he doesn't want me, or the pack, to know he's there. They've lived here my entire life, and know when someone is peeing in my yard. The mailman, I think, is yours too. While he's good at striking up a conversation, there is really no reason he needs to come all the way up here to tell me that I have no mail. Also, the driver that comes and brings my work supplies hasn't any idea what he's doing when he gets here. Much less what he's delivering to me. The company that I use, they should have let you know that I don't talk when I'm working...they should bring my stuff and go. Then there is also a woman that has rented out the building across the street from Running Water, and another one that is waiting tables at the local diner. Again, they need to be better at blending in by knowing the way things are done. They shouldn't order unsweet tea when they're in the south. Grits are a way of life here, and if they work in the area, they shouldn't turn up their noses at them. And no one, but no one that's from around here, wears combat boots under their jeans. It's always the little things that give you away."

Storm couldn't help it, she burst out laughing. She'd have to tell her men that they'd been found out, and the reasons why. Not only had she gotten them all, but she'd even given her the reasons that she'd caught on. Storm might have been able to point those things out to them had she been here, but she'd sent them in without briefing them.

When the two of them made their way to the large dining room where Bri and Andi were getting dinner set up, Brooke asked her if she had a moment. Storm told her that she had all the time in the world for family. They moved into an office that reminded her of her dad's office, which was now Riordan's. Well-appointed, with large windows that brought in all the outdoor light anyone could ever want.

"Brody, is he all right? I know from Darcy that you saved him. And I thank you for that, but he's the only person in the world I have left in my family...at least one that I love." Storm sat down on the large leather overstuffed couch and sighed. "Yeah, isn't that the most comfortable thing in the world? Grandda had it built for this room. He had the men bring out the stuff to make it and put it together right here for him. I think he about drove them insane with all of his questions and suggestions."

"If I thought I could get it out of here, you might find it missing when we leave." Brooke smiled, but it was strained and sad. "Brody is currently in France. I have a friend that has a lovely home there, and Brody has agreed to stay put so that we don't have to worry about him getting hurt by Blake and Benson. Were you aware that they have hurt him before?"

"Not until after Grandda got sick. I mean, he didn't really spend a lot of time here...Brody hates people. Hate is the wrong word, but he suffers from SAD. You know what that is?" Storm did and told her what she knew. "He has it bad, and it doesn't help that Uncle Blake and Benson make it worse when they're around him. But he's all right then? I mean, he gets very nervous when he can't breathe, as he calls it."

"I understand that. Yes, he is still there. I know that he has the ability to disappear, but he promised me, to keep you safe too, that he'd not leave the grounds. And there is plenty for him to roam. A vinery is there, as well as a stocked pond and a staff. He's going to be just fine while there."

Brooke nodded and picked up a small piece of pottery and held it in her hands. Comfort, Storm would bet. Brooke would feel connected holding onto something like that.

Storm looked around the room. That was when it hit her.

There were no other pieces of pottery in the room. And now that she thought about it, she'd not seen any in the entire house. It was as if someone had come in and—

"Have you been robbed by Blake and Benson?" Brooke asked her what she meant. "Your pieces. I'm assuming that you have a great many by you and your grandda. Yet there is not one piece here but the one in your hand."

"They're in Daniel's Cave." Storm asked her what that was. "Come on and I'll show you. It's under the shed. Grandda and I...well, it was either do something to protect our pieces or have nothing, the way that the two of them kept getting in the house all the time. So we and the pack built the building out there with the sole purpose of hiding the other works of art."

They made their way out to the shed, but to call it that was nuts. The thing looked like you could house planes in it. But as soon as they entered the cavernous building, Storm could see why they needed something so huge.

This was a building for a very large and successful business that not only shipped, but manufactured things as well. There was a place where the clay was stored, a shipping area that was stacked with long boards for making crates, and large scales to weigh them on. A medium sized forklift stood in one corner, beaten and worn, but she'd bet in tip top shape. Rolls of bubble wrap hung from the walls, along with rolls of brown craft paper and stacks of boxes that had yet to be shaped.

There were several wheels, all of them muddy, but again, in good shape. Storm walked around the room, marveling at what was needed to run Brooke's business, and even laughed when she saw vending machines, as well as a tea maker and a large fridge.

"You could almost live out here." Brooke pointed to the stairs and told her there were two bedrooms should someone need them. And that even with the large house, there wasn't enough room sometimes when they had a firing party. "Christ, woman, you're very organized. But then I would guess you'd have to be. By the way, I'm in love with this place."

Going to the bathroom, Brooke showed her the shower stall. It had been tiled with broken pieces of pottery, she told her, which had been kept for the sole purpose of doing just this. The three walls were bright and beautifully done with no seeming design, but just pieces put in grout because it fit. But when Brooke pushed on the smallest of the walls there was a small clicking sound before the door slid free. That was when she saw that it also had a second purpose. It hid the way to a sublevel.

"I took Darcy down here yesterday. I don't think he wanted to leave. Just be careful of the steps. Sometimes they can be a little damp." When they were at the bottom of the stairs, a light was turned on. Storm could only stare. "The pack helped us with it or we might not have been able to keep it a secret like we did. Not just with the building, which we couldn't have done without them, but also with bringing this down here. The shelves were something I wasn't sure that we'd want, but Grandda said that it was silly to have these things just lying on the ground everywhere. So over the course of the building going up, a crew worked down here putting shelf after shelf together until we had what you see here. It took us about six months to do it, but I think it turned out really well."

There were literally thousands of pieces of pottery. Some of them as tall as her, others small enough to fit in the palm of her hand. And everywhere she looked, Storm could see that each piece had been marked with a tag. The maker, date, and what it was called had been written on a sheet of paper, then laminated. Storm looked at a piece that had been made in the late fifties, and wondered not for the first time how anyone could be so talented and not let anyone know who they were.

"He loved what he did, my grandda. It wasn't just the making of the piece, but seeing it completed. It wasn't necessary for him to sell every piece. In fact, I think it hurt him to part with them at times. He told me once that it was much akin to putting your child out there to be criticized or praised by unknown forces. I think that he enjoyed people mostly because they had no idea that he was the artist of whatever piece they were asking him about." Storm asked her how she felt about them. "The only piece that I wish I'd never sold was my very first show piece. I was young...I think I was about twelve by then. I wanted to keep it forever. But the money went a long way in getting me established. We had money, plenty of it, but I needed my own things, my own tools and clay. Grandda understood that more than anyone, I think."

"This is amazing, Brooke. Not just that you've been able to preserve a very wonderful piece of history, but that you can come down here and be with him in a way." Brooke nodded and turned away. Storm didn't blame her for being emotional, she felt it too. "I wish I could have known him. Even a little. And I have to tell you, while I didn't know him, I'm betting that he'd be very proud of you right now."

"He would have been. And I think he would have approved of Darcy too. The rest of you...I'm not sure. He didn't care to share his mountain much, but he would have gotten a kick out of you seeing his work here." She grinned at her then. "You he would have loved. Strong women thrilled him to no end when they got their feathers up, as he called it."

As they made their way back to the upper levels, Storm asked Brooke what her plans were now. As far as Storm could see, she needed to be here as much as she needed to breathe.

This was her. The mountain, the air...hell, even the southern style that was a part of this world.

"Darcy said that he could gladly live here and never leave. I mean, he said he'd go to see you all when he could, but this is where he wants to be." Storm could see that of Darcy. He loved this place as much as Brooke did. "I think he'll be bored soon, don't you?"

"No. Not ever. Not only because you're here, but because Darcy loves home life. I think, of all the Harrison men, he's the best suited to live in this kind of environment. He loves it here. It's not only written on every part of his body, but when he's showing one of us something, be it the tree lined mountain or the kiln that you and your family made, he is proud to be here and be your mate." Brooke said that he just loved it right now. "No, he won't want to leave here. He loves you, Brooke. I don't know if he's told you that or not, but he does. And I think you might just be in love with him as well. Besides, it suits you both to be a part of this mountain. I think this is the perfect place for the two of you. So long as we can come and visit you once in a while."

"It isn't as bad as I thought it would be, having you all here." Storm laughed. "They don't do anything by half measures, do they? They fight loudly and love fully. And having them all together like this, you can see who the real ruler is. Mr. Harrison does as well. Mrs. Harrison, Bri, she is the quiet, do it my way sort of woman that can scare the stuffing right out of you and smile about it."

"Yes, that's the way of the Harrisons and Mom. And when one of us needs help, as you do, then we're right there too." Brooke nodded. "Your family, they're going to make things hard for you now. Harder than they did before, and will be less inclined to be nice about. Not that they were before, but now they're not going to hold back."

"I know. I wish it was different, but at this point, I don't care anymore. They've made their beds. And so long as Brody is safe and unharmed, I don't care what happens to Benson and Uncle Blake. I'm finished with them." For some reason Storm believed her. If they were killed, and they more than likely would be, then she thought that Brooke would be sad but not overly hurt about their passing. "Thank you, Storm, for all your help."

Storm wondered what she'd say when she found out what she knew of her father's death. But that was for later, after Christmas. Which, she remembered, was in two days, and they still hadn't gotten a tree. Brooke laughed and told her to go up the mountain, there were plenty to choose from. Storm thought she could easily have Christmas here every year. And then wondered if it was possible. She'd have to talk to Darcy about it later. After this was finished.

CHAPTER 7

Brooke made her way to the kitchen, still rubbing sleep out of her eyes. The house was quiet for having so many people in it. And she decided that she kind of liked having the Harrison family here. Not all the time, but to come en masse for a visit. Entering the kitchen, she stopped when she saw who was sitting at her table. She rubbed her eyes again just to make sure that what she was seeing was correct.

Walking to the fridge to get some tea, she thought about what was going on. Nikki was sitting in one of the chairs, her gun sitting on the table, with a cup of tea beside her hand. There were scones on the table as well…blueberry if she was smelling right. Andi was standing at the counter making… well, she thought it was biscuits, but sugar was being put on them so she wasn't sure. And then there was Thomas.

His face was a mess, scratches all over it, his lip bleeding. And his clothing looked like he'd dressed in the dark, buttons all askew and his hair mussed up. Nothing like the man who had come to irritate her to no end. Taking a drink of the cold tea before speaking, she asked Nikki if she was going into town later with her as they'd planned last night.

"We are. Storm said you knew a couple of places to get some good discounts on a few things on my list. A knife store?" Brooke nodded and told her there were several of those, as well

111

as a camping store and a kitchen place. "Yeah, that's where we need to hit too. Mom has a few people she wants to get some cast iron for. I think I heard the men were going to join us later, that they had a few things to take care of as well."

"Good. That's good." Andi handed her a warm biscuit, and she realized that whatever else she was making was going to be a huge breakfast for the family. The woman oozed homemaker. "So, is Thomas going to be joining us? I have to tell you, I don't think his momma is gonna be happy with him, dressed like he is. She's pretty fussy about everything, but Thomas will need to clean up some, if he's joining us."

"Yeah, about that. I found him on the property. I'm assuming that you have a few acres here." Brooke told her just over two thousand. "Wow, impressive. Anyway, so that tells me that he didn't just sort of wander on the wrong side of the fence, doing what he was. And because you noticed his mode of dress, I'll have to tell you that I had little to do with that. He fell in his...he fell."

Thomas whimpered but said nothing. Brooke noticed then, when she sat down in one of the other chairs, that his hands were tied to the chair with strips of plastic. Something was going on here and she'd play along with Nikki. For now. It was sort of funny really, to have this surreal conversation about a man who was sitting right there for her to ask should she want to. Sipping her tea and eating a second biscuit, Brooke waited. It was Thomas that spoke first.

"I told you, I thought you was gonna hurt me. I came here to talk to my intended." Nikki slammed her fist on the table, and both Brooke and Thomas jumped. "She won't pick out a ring with me. I can get a discount if she comes in with me. Momma isn't gonna be happy with me or you when she hears of this. Don't tell her, please. I can't let her know again."

"You were told, I'm assuming, that she's not going to be your anything, correct?" Thomas looked at her, then shook his head at Nikki. "No one told you that she was marrying my brother-in-law? I find that hard to believe. Besides, what you were doing when I found you does not make me think you'd make a good husband for Brooke. She likes a real man. Is it your momma that is making you do this, coming here to bother Brooke?"

"I'm a real man." The fist came down again; this time Brooke didn't jump, but Thomas started sobbing. "Mother said that Brooke would be a good match for me. Said that we'd have to make it a big deal to make sure that no one remembered me from before. I need her to come with me so that we can get it done and Momma will be happy with me again."

"What were you doing on the property, Thomas? I've told you several times that you're not to come here again." He cried harder and she looked at Nikki. "What did you catch him doing?"

"He was with one of those blow up dolls." It took Brooke a few seconds to realize what she meant. "Thomas here claims that he was only putting it in his car. I don't think that's what he was doing, since it was out of the box and filled with air. And other things I guess." The last part was said under her breath, so Brooke wasn't entirely sure she'd heard her right. Brooke looked at Thomas.

"Thomas, do you have sex with girly dolls?" Nikki cleared her throat and corrected her. "Oh. Oh my. A male blow up doll? You were having.... The male doll was.... Thomas, does your mother know?"

"I don't know what she's talking about. I was merely putting it in my car when she came out of nowhere and knocked me to the ground and hurt me." Thomas started sobbing again.

"I didn't do anything to it or to her."

"Your pants were down around your ankles and your dick was inside the thing. If you were merely putting it in your car, as you said, then why the fuck were you pounding that thing with your dick like you were planting potatoes with it?" Andi burst out laughing and Brooke had to fight hard not to join her. "Christ man, no one cares if you're gay or not. But don't fucking lie about it. And for Christ's sake, find a person, not some doll that is going to give you rubber burns."

Poor Thomas. After thinking about it—not him with the doll, but other things that he'd said—Brooke wondered why it had never occurred to her before that he was a homosexual. Not that his sexual preference bothered her, but apparently it did his momma. Also how he had hinted over the last weeks that this marrying thing was his momma's idea. And then she remembered the ring conversation and the discount he might have gotten. Mr. Gravely knew.

"Mother is going to be so unhappy about this." Brooke knew in that moment that he was a gay man who was terrified of his own mother. "She told me I just needed a wife. Someone that could.... I don't want to marry you, Brooke. I like you enough, but you're not what I want in a woman. Not any woman, but you were pretty enough. It was Momma that said I need a wife. To not have people remembering the other time."

"What you need is to get out of your mother's home and find a place of your own. I'd probably start by leaving the state. She's not a nice person if she doesn't let you be who you are." Thomas said she only wanted the best for him. "Well, if that were true then you'd be happily shacked up with someone more your type, not irritating the shit out of me trying to get me to marry you."

He cried more, and when Nikki got up and pulled out a

knife, he started screaming for her not to kill him. When she cut the plastic at his wrists, he put his hands on his face and cried all the harder. The poor man was beaten, she thought.

When he was finished, or at least not crying so hard, she asked him to look at her. He really was a mess. Brooke wondered what had happened to him, but decided that whatever it was, it might be the best thing for the poor man.

"Do you have any money, Thomas?" He said that his mother took his checks to pay bills and save for their wedding. "I think we both know now that's not going to happen. But here is what I want you to do. I'm going to give you some cash, and I want you to get in your truck and leave here. Not just my house, but Tennessee all together. Find a nice place to live and start doing just that. Living. You have to do this or...or I'm going to press charges. You know that is only gonna make your momma madder at you, don't you?"

"But she'll be so upset with me. You know how she can be." Brooke did know, but Mrs. Sheppard didn't scare her as much as she apparently did her son. "How will I know what to do?"

"You're a grown man. And you should have been out a long time ago. Your mom is holding you back." Brooke watched Nikki as she pulled out a notebook and started going through it. "Okay. I have just the place for you to go. Mark is a good friend of mine and he helps people acclimate themselves to the world. He usually works with trauma patients, but I think you're about as trauma affected as anyone else he might work with, and he'll help you out."

After making a few phone calls—and one of the Harrison men lending him some things to get him looking less like he'd been knocked around in the mud and more like a man on a mission—Thomas was ready to be on his way. He'd showered

115

and shaved, gotten his cuts fixed up, and been fed as well. He looked like a man who was determined to make this work. He looked at her before starting the truck.

"You'll talk to Momma for me?" She nodded and told him she'd take care of her. "I don't know how to thank you all for this. I've been...I'm just so sorry for all this, honey.... Sorry, Brooke. I'll pay you back when I get a job." Brooke told him not to worry about it. "I think you might have saved us both. You wouldn't have liked being married to me any more than I think I would have been to you."

"No, just you. Had you kept it up, I would have had to kill you." He laughed and she didn't. "Don't come back here, Thomas. Not for any reason. It's not that I wouldn't welcome you as a friend, but you return and she's going to drag you back under her thumb. You've been there much too long as it is."

"I know." He looked out the front of his truck and she turned to see Darcy there waiting. "He's a good man. And loves you very much. When he was fixing my lip, he told me that a lot of people would have had me arrested. You were giving me a rare thing in helping me get my shit together. His words, not mine. I swear to you, I'm not going to let her rule me anymore. I can't. Be someone that I'm not."

"Good. You deserve a second chance, so don't fuck it up. Darcy is right. I have enough crap going on in my life right now, and you were a part of the stuff I didn't want to have to deal with." Thomas asked her if it was her family. "Yes. Uncle Blake and Benson, they want what Grandda left me."

"Don't give it to them, Brooke. I loved your grandfather. You're a great deal like him in that you help those that need it. But I think he was a little kinder to me." She laughed with him, but was sad too. "I'm not coming back, I promise you. But

I will send you a postcard from time to time. I really am sorry about everything."

"Me too." Brooke watched him pull out of her drive. By nightfall he'd be in a safe place with good people. When arms wrapped around her from behind, she leaned back against Darcy when he kissed her shoulder. "He's going to be just fine."

"He will be now." She nodded. "Are you ready for this? Shopping with my family can be daunting. I know that from experience."

"How bad could it be? We hit a few shops, come back here, eat, and then I work for a while." Darcy just laughed. "Really, how hard can it be?" He was still laughing when they went in the house to get ready.

~~~

Darcy had been standing at the counter for ten minutes, and he was starting to get a little pissed off. Okay, he was a lot pissed off, he thought. Where the hell was the clerk? His dad came to stand beside him as he looked around again for someone to help him.

"I don't think you're gonna find her a ring in here." He told his dad he was beginning to see that. "No, what I mean is, these are diamonds and such. I don't think that's what she'd like."

He looked at his dad. "Why would you think that? I mean, I'm not saying you're not right, but what makes you come to that conclusion?"

"She wear diamonds and rubies now? Or have you seen any of them around her place? I'm assuming that you're sharing a room. She got anything fancy there?" Darcy said she didn't wear much of any jewelry, as a matter of fact. "Wanna know why?"

117

Darcy left with his dad. They were standing on the sidewalk when he saw the little shop across the street from where they were. Crossing when they could, not when the light told them to but when it was clear, they were in front of the store as the heavy traffic flowed by them. All he could think about was no wonder Brooke never came to town. It was a flipping madhouse.

Entering the store, Darcy asked his dad why he thought Brooke didn't wear jewelry. He knew for a fact that if his dad wanted to know something he'd find out in no time, and why Brooke didn't wear jewelry would be easy for him. Darcy asked him again what he'd found out.

"I didn't ask her, not right out, but she told your mom that she can't wear pretty things because when she's leaning into the kiln, it heats jewelry up and it burns her something terrible." Darcy paused in putting a blown glass fish back on the shelf and turned to look at his dad. "Telling you the truth. Bri said she's got a few scars on her neck when she wore some dangling kind of earrings while working. Brooke said that she hated to part with them, but it was just dangerous to risk getting burnt up to look nice to throw pots."

"I'm not even going to ask you how this conversation came up. But I guess that makes sense. What it doesn't do for me, however, is tell me what sort of ring I get her to ask her to marry me." He looked around the shop, loving the displays as well as all the items in it. There was a bit for everyone, and even some antiques on the shelves. "I guess I could find her something she can wear when we're together. I don't...."

He looked at the display of old jewelry. Moving closer to the case to get a good look, he saw the brooch lying in a basket lined with velvet. He asked to see it. When the elderly woman took it out and gave it to him, he knew immediately who he wanted to give it to.

"Your momma will love that." He nodded. "Does it have a place to put a picture? I'm telling you right now, if it does, I have the perfect one to put in it. Me and her on our first date, or the one of all you boys that was taken at Riordan's wedding. She'd sure love that."

Opening the small clasp, he saw that it had a place for two pictures. And on the back it had a pin and small loop. He asked the woman what it was for.

"Sometimes it wasn't feasible for a woman to be pinned up. Either the dress would have been snagged or the neckline just a little too lightweight to carry it off. So the hook was put on the back of it to wear as a necklace. See?" She pulled the chain that went with it from the bottom of the basket and put it in the loop. "I'm not sure this is the chain that goes with it, but when I bought it that was with it. You want it, I'll even wrap it up real pretty for you."

"I'll take it." He handed it back to her. "And if you could wrap it, I'd really appreciate it. But I could also use your help. I want to propose to someone, but I don't think...well, I don't think a ring is something that she'd like. Do you have any ideas?"

Her face turned as red as the velvet that the brooch had been sitting on before she spoke. "You're that man, the one that is up there with Running Water, aren't you? My husband, he's Morgan Boyer. I'm Pauline, his mate."

"Yes, I'm Darcy Harrison. It's a pleasure to meet you. This is my dad, Ordan. My family is here for Christmas and to bring in the New Year with us." He shook her hand. "He and the pack, they've taken very good care of her. And I hope that they continue. It's nice to know that they're there when I can't be."

"She lets us run when we want. Pack meetings are held up

there too. Her grandda was about the nicest man there was, but I'm telling you, it does my heart some good to know that she's got someone now. Brody is a good boy, but he doesn't have heart like she does. And them other two need to be shot and buried so that they're never found." She told him she'd be right back. But she continued talking as she made her way past a dark heavy curtain in the back of the shop. "I do love that girl like my own. But like I was saying, you want to watch out for her uncle and the boy, Benson. He's not got a good bone in his whole body. Neither of them do."

He heard a crash and asked if she was all right. When she assured him that she was, he looked around the shop again. That was when he found the for sale sign.

It was old and faded. The phone number on it was marked out several times to be replaced with another one. The newest number looked like it was fresh. Not having any way of knowing for sure, when Mrs. Boyer came from the back room, he asked her about it.

"Morgan and I want to retire somewhere there isn't a mountain. While we love it here, we're just too old to get up and down it, even on our best days. Here you go." She handed him an old cigar box. "Right after her momma passed on, poor thing, Daniel, he came in here so broken hearted that I nearly wept with him. Said that someone had taken his wife's jewelry box and all the things she'd saved. Then he asked me if I'd keep an eye out for some of the pieces. Never thought in all my life I'd ever find any of them, but lo and behold, here these came in a month or so later. Daniel asked me to hold onto them for a bit. Never did come to get them, but told me to hold them for him every time I asked. He paid for them, even gave me a little each month to keep them in the back room. But he never asked for them until a few days before he passed on."

Darcy opened the box up and looked at the array of pieces in it. There were very expensive items lying right next to cheap costume jewelry. But the thing that caught his eye was the hair comb. It was old, probably older than the woman in front of him. Pulling it out, he realized that there were two of them, and they were beautiful.

"Her momma's. Brooklynn didn't wear much jewelry, not because they couldn't afford them, but she wasn't showy, not like them boys. But she did wear those every time I saw her." She pulled out the watch that was old as well and no longer working. "I had it looked at; won't take much to get it running, just a cleanup. If you want, I can have my friend fix it today and get it up to the mountain for you."

"Yes. Please." He looked around the shop and then back at Pauline. "How much? For all of it?"

"You thinking of becoming a shop owner, Darcy?" He nodded and smiled at her. "Well then, it's yours."

"Oh no, I'll buy it from you. And the inventory." She just laughed. "I don't understand. I really would like to purchase this place from you."

"You own it just as much as little Brooke does now, being her mate and all." He asked her what she meant. "Brooke, she owns this building and the ones on either side. She told me when I asked her about closing up that she wanted to put it on the market. Told me right off that if I closed up shop, she wanted to sell the buildings. Not the only one she owns in town either…has her fingers in a great many things in this town if you want to know the truth of it. And what she don't have in the way of stores, she owns the land it sits on. We made a deal that I'd stay until someone came in and bought me out. You did me a favor."

"What about the inventory?" She looked around when he

did. "You can't just let it go with the store. I mean, there has to be a lot of money invested in this place. Not to mention, I can see bags and other items you had to purchase just to be in business as well."

"I'm done, son. And this other stuff, just more things that I'd have to pack up should I shut the doors on it all. I loved it when I was younger; hell, my own kids worked right here with me, learning how to count by taking money from tourists right along with learning to read from labels and such. I've not gotten anything new for here in ten years or so. Figured it was gonna be sold up and I didn't want to have to pack it away. You take it, make a good showing of it, and I'll be a happy woman."

Darcy spent the next hour going over what needed to be done to take over. Pauline told him that most of the shops shut up on January first, then didn't reopen until late March or so. She told him that she'd stay on until she closed up, then she was finished. He even made a deal with her to take what she wanted out of the place, and all the money for the rest of the month was hers to take. It probably wouldn't be much, but that was all she'd take in the form of a payment. Leaving the store with his dad, Darcy felt better than he had in a long time about life in general.

"Well, just talked to your mom. She and the girls are having lunch at one of them all you can eat places, and we're to meet them there if we're hungry." Darcy said he could eat. "Yeah, me too. Oh, and I'd like to buy a few things in there too, if you've a mind to sell them. I'll come back after we eat. Found a pretty knife that I think Nikki would like. And a couple of little things that Mac might want. I think they're Brooke's granddda's, but I can't tell without help."

Darcy reached out to Brooke, and wasn't surprised to find

that she was exhausted. He laughed a little when she told him he was going to die when they got home. He asked her if she was having fun.

I guess. But there are people here. He told her it was a tourist town. *Yes, I get that, but I forgot how many there were. And your mother? Christ, she'd shop until you dropped, then just drag you along behind her, going on about sales and getting a good deal. I might take her to one of my gallery openings. She might be able to get me a better deal on their cut of sales. She sure can haggle with the best of them.*

We're coming to meet you at the restaurant. I hope you don't mind. She told him that they were nearly there and could see his brothers already sitting outside. *I wanted to tell you what I just did. I hope it doesn't make you mad at me, but I'm going to take over Serendipity. I talked to Pauline, and she's glad to be rid of it.*

Why on earth would I be mad at you for that? Besides, she's been trying to get me to take it from her for a month now. I kept meaning to go and talk to her, but I've been dealing with...I've been having my own issues. I'm sure she understands, but I was hurting too much to talk to her. Darcy assured her that Pauline understood and wasn't the least bit mad. *You thinking of running it like it is?*

A little. She left the inventory, and I'm going to keep most of it. But I want to see about putting some smaller things in it, things that a tourist could carry out without too much trouble. He was warming to the idea, and smiled when she asked him if he'd thought of pottery. *I might have to find me a potter. I don't suppose you know of one that might be interested in giving me a good discount on things? And Dad thinks there might be a few pieces in there anyway. Do you know if they are either of yours?*

If they're little vases with a mountain on them, then yes, they're Grandda's. He put a few pieces in there a long time ago, and would check to see if she needed more of them from time to time. But lately

123

I think she just told him not to stock them. She hasn't wanted to deal with people any more than I do. He said he could see that, and was going to let his dad take them. *He can come by Daniel's Cave too, if he wants something for Mac. I'm sure we can find something for him.*

He told her that he'd talk to his dad and was sure he'd love that. But that he might want to clean her out of her work.

Darcy was still laughing when he and Dad crossed the street a block from the restaurant. He could see his family there, all of them standing in a tight circle like wagons ready for battle. Just as he was ready to call out to them, he saw Blake. And coming from the other side of the car they were in was Benson.

Darcy wasn't sure that they'd seen Brooke yet—his family had her pretty well sheltered, and he didn't want to alarm her if she hadn't seen them. So, reaching for Riordan, Darcy knew that he'd keep her safe until he got there. It was the longest walk he'd ever made getting to his mate.

CHAPTER 8

Riordan told Darcy that he could see them. Telling Storm might have been a mistake, but he wanted her to be on alert too. He knew that she was armed...he was pretty sure that they all were except for Mom and Brooke. But when Brooke turned and looked in the direction the family was, Riordan reached out to touch her hand to stop her from going after them. Brooke looked at him for a second before turning to her uncle and brother again.

"Darcy is coming, and he would like for you to stay with us until he gets here. He said that he'd like to be here when you deal with them." Not what he said exactly, but it was close enough. The man had begged him to not let her go to them alone. "See him right there? He's with my dad."

"They're going to fuck things up for us. Not Darcy, but my brother and Blake, aren't they?" He told her only if she let them. Riordan knew what type of men her brother and uncle were. Greedy fucks who thought everything they wanted should be theirs. "Don't let Darcy get hurt, all right? I've sort of grown fond of him over the last few days. He sort of grows on you like fungus, doesn't he?"

"Sort of. But you shouldn't let them hurt you either, if you can help it." She nodded and waited for Darcy without taking her eyes off the other two.

When Darcy got to her, he held her hand and Riordan watched the two men. He saw when they realized that Brooke was with them and they started toward their group. Storm stepped between them and Brooke. This might be bad. Really bad.

"Hello, fuck turds. You doing a little shopping? Must not have a lot of people to buy for…you don't have a single bag." Brooke stood next to Storm but didn't get any closer to them. Riordan was ready, his gun at his side. He'd learned the hard way that you couldn't pull it fast enough if someone wanted you shot. It had nearly cost him his life when he'd thought the person would never shoot him.

"We wanna talk to Brooke." Blake looked at his niece and smiled, showing all his teeth. Riordan wondered if he thought he was being reassuring or if he knew he was fucking scary looking. "Come on now, it's nearly Christmas, Brooke, honey. Don't you want to hang out with your blood relatives? Why don't you come along with us now? Then we'll talk about some things that we left unfinished."

"What would that have been? Last time I talked to you face to face, you tried to break into my home and rob me." Brooke turned to her brother then. "And you? Let me see. Oh yeah, I remember now. You came to an opening and broke a piece of my work when you decided that I was either going to pay you or you'd make me. You broke Brody's arm, you fucking prick. Then, if I remember correctly, you spent the next forty-eight hours in jail, didn't you? How did that work out for you? Either of you?"

Storm took a step back and smiled at him. *I think she has this, don't you?* Riordan nodded. *I'm almost glad she's not armed. I'm pretty sure she might have killed them both already.*

I think you might be right. But I'm also thinking it might not hurt for her to be armed. At least until this thing is over. Storm said she'd look into getting her something she could handle. *Storm, she reminds me of you. A little.*

That earned him a smile and a quick kiss on the mouth. Christ, Riordan loved his wife. But then Benson started talking and Riordan needed to pay attention. Just in case he had to tell someone what happened when Brooke or Darcy killed them.

"You need to give us some money, Brooke. I'm telling you right now, this ain't no way to treat your family. Just give us enough to get by on and we'll leave you alone for now." Brooke laughed and Blake looked like he was going to hit her. But Darcy stood behind her. "You're really brave when you got somebody around to take care of you. But you won't always have them. What do you think is going to happen when they go home? They will you know. City people can't live like we do."

"City people? I don't think they're much different than anyone else. With the exception of you. You're a bastard. And I'm pretty sure that they've never stolen a thing in their lives, like you have. Nor have they murdered someone just for the thrill of it. Knocked someone up just because they didn't feel like wearing a condom." Blake doubled up his fist, but before he could draw back to no doubt hit her, she hit him right in the face with her own fist. Riordan burst out laughing when the man hit the ground. "I'm not ten anymore, Blake, and you might want to remember that in the future, if you have one. I will not take you knocking me around or putting me in dark caves again. Never."

When Blake reached behind him, five guns were pointed at him before he could pull out whatever he had. Darcy reached down, pulled the gun away from Blake, and handed it to Storm. Riordan was never so relieved to have his family with him as he was right at that moment. This might not have ended well had they not been there.

"What did you plan to do with that, Blake? Shoot her?" Darcy looked over at Benson, who had his hands up and didn't move. "You…you thinking of killing her too? I have news for you…you even try to hurt her and I will come after you. As I've told you before, no one will know where your body is when I'm finished with your sorry asses."

"We need some money, we got nothing. Great Grandda didn't leave us anything at all like we thought he would. How the hell are we gonna get anything if we don't have some of what she's got? I already asked her nicely for some of the pieces she's got up in that house. Told me to fuck off." Riordan took a step back when his mom slapped Benson in the face. "What the hell was that for?"

"You'll watch your language, young man, or I'll be taking you to the woodshed myself." Benson seemed confused and looked at Riordan. But Mom apparently wasn't finished with him yet, and jerked his chin around so that he faced her again. "You'll tell these ladies that you're sorry, or so help me, I'll make you that way."

Rubbing his cheek, Benson looked as confused as ever. Brooke finally spoke to him, explaining what his mom meant about making him sorry if he didn't say he was sorry to them.

"For cussing? Well, that's not going to happen. I'm not sorry for doing no such thing." His mom tapped her foot, and each of his brothers and Riordan knew what that meant. A whooping was going to happen, but none of them were in the line of fire. This time. "Listen here, old broad, you can't tell me what to do. I'm not your fucking kid. And even if I was, I'd not—"

The gun was in his mouth before he could finish the

DARCY

sentence. He knew that his mom had been taking lessons from Storm. She'd told him that his mom was an excellent shot and very calm during her practice. Seeing her now, holding the gun with her hand as steady as ever while she made Benson eat it, Riordan wondered if she needed to take any more lessons. She was kinda scary. Oh hell, she was very scary.

"You're lucky that I'm in a very good mood, young man." He nodded when she asked him if she looked like she was. "I am. Now, you're going to tell us that you're sorry for messing up our fine day, gather up your uncle before someone kills him, and leave us alone. I've had about enough of your rudeness for one day. If I take this gun out and you don't satisfy me, I will shoot you. You can take that to the bank, as I've heard my Ordan say before. And in the event that you didn't know this about me, I'm a woman of my word."

As soon as the gun was out of his mouth, Benson looked like he might attack. It would be his last mistake of many, Riordan was sure. None of them, his dad included, had lowered their weapons, and Benson had to see that he was outgunned, not to mention outmanned. But then he was an idiot, and more than likely figured he could not only outrun a bullet but come out of this unscathed.

"Boy, you say you're sorry to any of them and I will quit you. You don't owe them a damned thing. They mean shit to us." Blake cried out when the gun that Liam had in his hand popped one shot between Blake's legs. "What the fuck is wrong with you people? This ain't got a damned thing to do with any of you."

"Actually, it has everything to do with us. She's my mate, as I have explained to you once before. I even told you that we're all tigers as well." Darcy looked at them before looking back at Blake. "This is my family. A family of tigers that will

129

fuck you up should you mess with any of us. The fact that we're being nice to you right now should in no way make you think that we'll be this way the next time we encounter you. Because that would be a mistake on your part. A deadly one."

Darcy turned to their mom and said he was sorry. "That's fine, son. Right now I could think of a few words myself that I'd like to spew on these two."

Riordan didn't say anything, but he did wonder why he was ever worried about his family when he wasn't around. They were better at protecting themselves than he might be. When Benson told Mom and the other women he was sorry, he simply walked away. Blake lay there for a few more seconds before he looked at Brooke.

"This here, it's not done between us. I hope you know that, Brooke. You owe me some of what you got, and I'm going to get it. Come hell or high water." She didn't bother saying anything to him. "I'm gonna get what I deserve."

Brooke laughed and Riordan wondered at her stress level. That was until she spoke.

"Oh, I have no doubt about that. I'm thinking, however, that what you really deserve and what you think you deserve won't be nearly the same thing." When she turned her back on her uncle, Riordan could have gladly picked her up and hugged her. Brooke was going to fit right in with his family, he thought, and he was glad to have gotten to know her better in this. "I'm really hungry. How about you guys?"

When she moved toward the front of the restaurant, Darcy turned to him with pride and disbelief on his face. When he smiled at him, Riordan laughed.

"I think I'm going to enjoy being her mate." Riordan told him he thought he'd be tamed in no time. "I hope so. I surely do. But she's right, I'm hungry. How about you?"

They just left Blake there. No one answered his threats, and there were plenty of them. Nor did anyone go back and hit him again, which he surely did deserve.

As soon as they were inside, their table being readied for them, Riordan pulled his mom into his arms and kissed her on the forehead.

"What was that for?" He told her that he loved her. "And I love you too. I have to admit, I was a little surprised by myself. But that man, he's going to be trouble, isn't he?"

"Yes." She nodded. "But I think they'll be able to handle him all right, don't you? I mean, she's not someone I'd tangle with. You either, for that matter. You are amazing."

"I am, aren't I? But no, she's not one to be tangled with, not on this. But I do worry." So would he. "And I'm going to miss them when we go. I'm thinking that he won't be talking her into coming to live near us, aren't you? And even if he did, she'd be so unhappy up where we are that she'd just wilt and fall apart. She needs to be here, with him."

"I think so too." He hugged Mom, telling her again that he loved her. "Maybe she'll let us come stay with her enough that we won't miss them so much. I think I could get used to this clean mountain air, how about you?"

"I hope so...I'm going to miss them. Even if they come to see us all the time, they're not right there. You know, across the street from us." He nodded, understanding more than she knew. Riordan was going to miss his little brother as well. "Maybe they'll give me lots of grandchildren that will come and stay with me. That might make it worth it."

When she walked away, he looked at Andi. She was just beginning to show a little bump from hers and Mac's child. Sometime in late June there would be a baby in the family. He wanted to tell his mom that he and Storm had decided to work on a couple themselves, but decided to wait until the time was right. Sitting with his family, Riordan thought there wasn't anything better than this.

~~~

Darcy and Ennis had been sent to find a tree. He wasn't sure what to do once they found one, but he was determined that it would be the biggest and best. What he'd not counted on, and should have, was that they were not going into a lot to get it, but up the mountain to cut one down themselves. Ennis stopped them by yet another pine tree and asked him what he thought.

"I don't know. It just doesn't say country Christmas, does it?" Ennis shook his head and they moved on. "I think I'd rather be doing this than trying to find ornaments in the attic. Did you see the amount of stuff up there?"

"It looks like someone had it organized, but you're right, there are a lot of boxes and things up there. How many trunks do you suppose are up there just waiting to be unearthed?" He said he had counted ten. "Ten? Shit, they're never going to find them, and we're going to have the most naked tree we've ever seen."

"Mom is taking two of the empty trunks back with her, I guess. Brooke said that she could have them when Mom asked about them. I guess she wants to give one to Andi for the baby's room." Darcy thought of the things he'd seen up there that had belonged to the children of the Rickson family. "That handmade cradle and bed, do you suppose that they'll clean up nice? I think I could almost see our children in them one day."

"You thinking of having children right away? I would be too if I found my mate, I guess. But damn, Brooke has got her shit together. More so than I think Storm or the rest of the women do in this family."

He was right about that. Everything had a place and was marked. He wondered aloud if he thought Brooke would help him organize the new shop.

"If she does then you'll be able to find everything without having to look too hard for it. But I'd hope that you'd take better care in what you have in yours. Christ, did you see some of the stuff a lot of those places are selling? Some of it is pure junk." He agreed with him and told him of his plans. "Also, I'd hate to be the one that goes through that back room with you. For as much as Brooke is organized, I don't think Pauline knew there was such a word. It's a mess."

"You're right. I'm going to start there, just to see what I have and work around that. Brooke has already said she'd put some of hers and her grandda's work in the place, so that'll be a good start. She said that she'd make something special for us too. Exclusive to the store." Ennis nodded and pointed to another group of trees. As they made their way to it, he continued. "No shirts, we've decided. And only a few bigger things that can be carried by hand. She said that we could pick up some suitcases too, use them as displays as well as sell them."

"Sounds good. I keep seeing them at some of the auctions that I go to. Maybe I can pick up a few of them for you cheap." Darcy thanked Ennis. "I think this is it."

It was. The tree was perfect. Taller than he'd been thinking, but beautiful all the same. When they walked around it twice, they knew that it was going to take a while to cut it down. Just before they pulled out the two saws they'd brought, Morgan and his son showed up on a four-wheeler. Darcy decided right then that he was going to see about getting one. It was nice and not too intrusive.

"You're going to be a while if you do it that way." All of them laughed when Brent, Morgan's youngest son, pulled out a chainsaw. "Brooke gives us permission to come up here and find a tree for our pack house. You don't mind, do you? We might have to sit down and talk about the things we did before and what you want from us now, I guess."

"No. Not at all. And if Brooke is happy with your arrangements, then so am I. Maybe you can tell me what some of them are sometime so I don't step on toes, but I don't want to change anything." Darcy looked at Morgan when Brent started the saw up and began cutting the tree. "You retiring so soon?"

"Yes. The new year will be bringing about changes for us. Brent is going to take over the pack, and Pauline and I are going on a little trip. One I think I've owed her for a great many years." Darcy told him congratulations. "No, it is you I must congratulate. You have given us so much."

As soon as the tree was downed, Brent and Morgan helped them tie it to the four-wheeler and drag it down the hill. Darcy was most definitely getting one of the vehicles as soon as he could.

Almost as soon as they were in sight of the house, about fifty or more wolves, all of them with something around their necks, came to greet them. Morgan didn't say anything, but laughed when Darcy paused.

"They'll never harm you and yours." Darcy nodded. "Come. It's time for you to meet the pack that roams your lands."

His family and Brooke came out of the house then and walked to where the pack was. When he pulled her into his arms she looked up at him, so disappointed looking that he held her tighter. She told him that she couldn't find the ornaments at all.

"Well, we'll think of something. We were sort of caught on short notice about this. Next year will be better." Morgan bowed before them and Darcy watched as the tree was carried into the house by some of the men of the pack. "Thank you for your help today. We'd still be up there if you and Brent hadn't come along."

"We planned it that way, young cat. Had you still been up there cutting it down, we would not have been able to give you our gift." Morgan nodded to his son and smiled at them. "In the tradition of our kind this holiday season, we have come to give you a gift of love and friendship. We know that it has been a great many years since any tree has been put into this home. We also know that the things to make the holiday bright for you and yours have long since been gone. Today, we wish to give you something in return for all that you've done for us. The holidays."

The first person to come to them was Brent. "I give you this gift of an ornament, made by my hand, to thank you for the loan you gave me to go to college. Without your help, I wouldn't have been able to study as much as I needed. Thank you."

The ornament was a large pinecone sprinkled with not just gold from the mountain streams, he told them, but with the gems that lay along the banks as well. A small signed picture of his diploma was given as well.

The next person was Pauline. "I give you this gift of not an ornament, but of the star to grace your tree. Without your help over the years with the loan to fill my store, there wouldn't have been any money for extras. A vacation with the children when they were younger. A new pair of skates for them when they asked. You two will be the stars of our family forever and a day."

Gift after gift was given to them, some of them fashioned from the things in the mountain, others made by their own hand. There were tiny knitted coats on pipe cleaner hangers that looked like Santa coats. Small sleds with miniature bags of handmade toys in them. Santas made of pinecones, others made of stones and dressed in scraps of material. Children also brought them candy canes made to look like reindeer, and stockings filled with cookies and peanut brittle.

Boxes had been brought out to put them in, and his mom took care that each of the ornaments was placed in them with care. When Morgan's turn came, he put out his hand and Darcy reached for it, only to have Brooke's hand put over his.

"This is what I have waited for since I first laid eyes on you, Running Water." He cleared his throat and nodded to his pack. "Many years ago, Daniel Rickson invited me to his home. It was going to be the birth of his great granddaughter, he told me. And even when the doctors, all of them men of books, told him it was a boy, he knew that it would be his greatest creation to date, one he told me later that he'd never be able to outdo, nor did he want to. And he was correct, as he usually was. When Brooke was but moments old, Daniel brought the babe out to let us see, and there he stood, a man sobbing about how he'd been given the greatest gift of all that day, and that he was proud to share it with the people of the mountain and earth."

Darcy looked at his parents when his dad put his hand on his shoulder. He was crying with Mom. Darcy was having a hard time holding his tears back as well. Morgan put his hand under his then, and continued with a speech that was from his heart. Darcy could almost feel the love he had for his mate.

"The month before he was to pass, he invited me to his home again. I had been here many times over the years, both

136

with great happiness and sadness. But this time, I went with the heaviest heart that I have ever had. I knew, as he did, that it was well past time for him to leave this mountain." Morgan asked his wife to join them. And when she laid her hands, one on the top and one on the bottom of theirs, Darcy felt the power of the great pair of wolves. "He asked me that day not to mourn him or his passing, but to celebrate it with life and love. He made me promise that should his darling little creation find happiness, I was to bless the union in his stead. To not just give them permission to wed, but that I was to help them on the journey as if he was there to do it for them. I was to give them what he knew he'd never be able to give. And this is it."

The band, scarlet in color and made of the finest wool, was wrapped around all their hands by Brent. The paws that were sewn into it were white, as pure as the falling snow, and they seemed to be walking in a line around the red, in a never-ending circle...like life, Darcy realized. When Brent stepped back, Darcy looked at Morgan and his mate.

"As pack leader, it is my honor and my privilege to unite this couple in the way of our kind. May you live a long and wonderful life, may you have children aplenty, and from this day forward, may your love for each other grow stronger daily and your friendship forever strengthen." He cleared his throat. "By the power vested in me by the state of Tennessee, I pronounce you man and wife, mate to mate, love to love."

"I'm sorry, what?" Morgan laughed at Brooke and kissed her on the cheek. "Did you just marry us?"

"I did. It was what your grandfather wanted of me, to be ordained and to be the one to see you on the next adventure of your life. He said he thought it would be one hell of a ride too." Morgan nudged him in the shoulder. "You can kiss your bride if you want."

Darcy looked at Brooke. They might be married or not, but he wasn't going to do anything until she said it was all right with her. When she looked up at him, Darcy could see that she was nervous. Leaning down to her ear, he told her that he loved her with all his heart, and if she wanted this, then he did as well.

"I love you too. I didn't want to, to be honest." Everyone laughed and her face heated. "What I meant was, I didn't want to fall in love with anyone. There have only been two men in my life that I loved, and they are both special. But to have you here, loving me the way that you do, I can't think of any better way of starting off the new year. As your wife."

Darcy pulled Brooke to him and kissed her. When he lifted his head and looked down at her face, Darcy knew for as long as he lived, this moment in time would be what kept him going. He loved her so very much that he wanted to shout it out to the world. Turning to the pack and his family, he lifted her up in his arms and held her to him.

"You all can decorate the tree; I'm going to take my new wife to bed." Everyone laughed and cheered for them. He looked at Morgan. "Are we married? Truly?"

"Yes. I promise you, you're man and wife. I filed the paperwork myself early this morning." Darcy headed for the house. "Congratulations, Mr. and Mrs. Harrison."

Darcy thought that was the best name he'd ever been called as he made his way to their bedroom. He had a wife. Darcy Harrison had a wife.

CHAPTER 9

She'd never been so nervous in all her life. But when Darcy kissed her, she felt her body warm to his, her heart pound in a way that wasn't like before they were married. When he lifted his head from hers and smiled, all she could think about was that her grandda would have loved him.

"I love you so very much." She told him she loved him as well. "This wasn't what I had in mind for a wedding day, but I can't think of anything more perfect."

"Do you think we should have waited? I mean, at least get the tree set up for tomorrow?" He just grinned at her as he took off his tee shirt and dropped it on the floor. "I mean, won't your family want to be with us?"

"I should hope not. What I plan to do to you isn't anything I want them to know about, much less see." She felt her face heat up and told him that's not what she meant. "I know, love, but they understand. And if they don't, I'm sure that they'll let us know. Tomorrow."

When he opened up the fly on his pants, she reached for his zipper and pulled it down as she watched his face. There was something so incredibly sexy about undressing him. She slipped her hand into his pants when she had the fly opened all the way, and wrapped her hand around his thickness.

"You are forever hard and ready, aren't you?" He told

her it was her fault. "How is the state of your cock my fault? Which, by the way, I think is the best part of you."

"Thanks, I think. But all I ever think about is sliding it into you. Bending you over a table or chair and fucking you until you scream. Then there is eating you. I love the way you scream out my name when you come. And my cat? Christ, he could devour you right now, he wants you so badly." She felt him purr along Darcy's skin. "Can you feel him there? Ready to take your cream into his mouth?"

"I love it when he licks me until I come. And when he slides his tongue into me, it's like being fucked with a large rough dildo. Just the thought of him doing that makes me wet and hot." He picked her up in his arms and she frowned at him. "I wasn't finished with you."

"Good, because I'm nowhere near finished with you either." Darcy put her on the edge of the bed and stood up. When he pulled his pants down to his knees, she wrapped her hand around his cock and pulled him to her. "I love it when you take me in your mouth."

She kissed the tip of his cock then licked him from tip to root. Cupping his balls in her hand, she took him into her mouth as deeply as she could, then swallowed when he rolled his hips. She wasn't sure if she could do this, but when he curled his hand in the back of her hair and fucked her slowly, Brooke thought she could gladly die with him taking her this way.

He fucked her throat over and over until she knew that he was close to coming. Cupping his balls again, she held them in her fingers, rolling them around, feeling the weight of them when he cried out. The first taste of his cum sliding down the back of her throat had her coming quickly, but it wasn't enough. When he pulled back, his cock still hard and stiff, she reached for him again only to have him back away.

"Turn around and lean on the bed." Getting up, she nearly fell when he tore her clothing off. No gentle stripping, he ripped them off. The sound of the material tearing in half had her body heating more, her pussy swelling to the point of pain. So when he pushed her to the bed, her ass up in the air, she slid her fingers into her pussy as he slammed his cock into her from behind.

"Vibrator?" It took her lust filled mind a moment to think of what he was saying. "Where is it? I want you to use it while I fuck you this way."

He reached into the drawer next to her side of the bed and nearly had her coming when he turned it on. Darcy never stopped fucking her. In fact, when he turned on her toy, she could swear that his cock thickened inside of her.

Darcy rubbed it over her ass, down her back, and over her shoulders. Instead of being relaxing, sort of like a massage, it brought her to the edge of reason until she was begging him to let her have it. When he pressed it against her sensitive clit, Brooke screamed. She came a second, then a third time, when he continued to hold it hard against her.

"Please, no more." That of course made him take her harder, pressing her deeper into the mattress until she was nearly bent in half. Still the vibrator touched off climax after climax until she could no longer stand up. When he pulled from her she fell to the bed, and he flipped her over to her back and dropped to his knees between her legs. "You have to let me rest. You've worn me out."

"Not yet. My cat wants you."

And suddenly the thick tongue of the cat was inside her. Brooke begged for him to stop between earth shattering releases, told him she was going to die, but he didn't stop.

And when he bit her in the thigh, tearing into her flesh, she didn't have the strength to cry out in pain...he'd really worn her out past exhaustion. It took her under like the lights had been snapped out.

When she woke he was curled around her, his cock still as hard as stone at her back. Brooke arched her body, rolling her ass over his cock. Darcy rolled her to her back, and she held him to her as he took her breast into his mouth and sucked hard.

"I love watching you sleep after I've fucked you senseless. But you left me hanging. My poor cock is hurting now, it's so in need of relief." He moved between her legs; his cock was indeed painfully hard looking. When she reached for him, thinking of fisting him until he came, he asked her to lay back and let him come all over her. "Then I'm going to fuck you until you're out again. Or I am. Whichever comes first."

"I don't think it will take much." He sat up on his knees and she leaned up on her elbows. Watching him fist his cock, seeing the cum drip off the tip, made her hungry to have him. Reaching for her vibrator that lay beside her, she turned it on low and pressed it gently to the underside of his cock.

"Christ, that's it." She rubbed it up and down his shaft, noting when he cried out and when he moved like it was painful. "More baby. Take me in your mouth while you do this."

Taking his cock into her mouth, she could feel the vibrations running along him. When she touched it to his balls, ever so gently, he cried out and tightened his grip on her hair. He fucked her hard, his cock taking her mouth in quick punches to her throat as he had her pussy before. Brooke knew the moment that he came, and felt him pull from her.

The spray was hot, touching her face, eyes, and lips. When

he pulled her body to his again, he came on her breasts, and her nipples dripped with his cum. And when he kissed her, she knew that he could taste himself on her mouth, and moaned when he laid her back on the bed and slid into her.

"Do you have any idea how much I love watching you play with yourself?" She wrapped her legs around him, the vibrator still in her hand rubbing along his ass and back. "I'm going to come. And when I do, I'm going to mark you again."

"Yes, Darcy, make me yours."

He came hard, his body nearly sliding into her he took her so deeply. And when he bit into her throat, tearing into her, she came with him, screaming out his name over and over until she passed out again.

~~~

Blake could not find either of his nephews. One he was going to use, the other he'd beat to crap. When he tried to call him yet again, he got the same voice offering to take a message for him. The fucker hadn't even set up his own voice mail but had used the canned one. Ending the call, Blake sat on the couch and thought.

Here it was the night before Christmas, and not only was he all alone, but he was also not going to be getting anything from anyone. Not from his grandda, nor that fucking cunt of a niece of his either. She was going to pay up or he was going to have to do something drastic again. The knock at the door had him jumping up and ready to tear into Benson when he opened it. But the man standing there had him backing up.

"Mr. Rickson?" He nodded at the man in the very expensive looking suit. "I have a few questions for you about the murder of William Graceson."

"He's...he was my brother-in-law." The man nodded and came into the apartment he'd been staying in as if he'd been invited. "I don't know why you'd be asking me questions... Will died some twenty-five years ago."

"Twenty-six this spring coming up." Blake nodded; he knew the date like it was his birthday. He even celebrated it like it was one when he had the funds. "Some new evidence has been brought forth, and I'm here to ask you a few questions. Also, so you know, my partner is looking into some other things that were found on the property of your niece, Brooke. I'm to understand that there is some bad blood between the two of you. Not just you and Brooke, but also her father. Something about her inheriting all the money and property from Daniel Rickson, your grandfather and her great grandfather."

"Just a misunderstanding between us. Nothing to have you get involved in." The man stared at him with a cocked brow. "What I mean is, she and I are working it out. I think we can come to an understanding soon. While she can be a bit stubborn at times, she does love her family."

"You think so? Not the way she tells it. You've been harassing her and her new husband too, haven't you? His family as well since they've been here. We heard all about how Darcy's momma took you to task. She's not one that I'd be messing with, that mother-in-law of hers." Blake pointed out that they weren't married. "Yes, they are. Just today as a matter of fact. Married up there on the land. Heard it was a sight to behold, too."

"No. No, that's not right. They can't be married. I would have heard about it." Blake tried to recall if anyone had tried to contact him about it, and couldn't remember anyone asking him or even hinting that they'd already wed. "She's just saying that to piss me off. Like I said, we're working things out, but she still likes to get a few digs in if she can."

"Why would that piss you off? You don't want her

happy?" What he wanted her to be was dead, but a husband in the picture was going to make her dying and him getting everything harder. "Anyway, she's married. Checked on the paperwork myself. Nice family too."

He wasn't going to think about Brooke fucking up his life by taking a husband. Blake had been planning things. Lots of different accidents could befall her before too much longer. There was going to be an explosion in her work shed and she'd die. Someone might get into her house and murder her in bed. Or her body would simply be dumped out in the open for some animal to get at her. The only way he could think of for him to get all the money and not just whatever he could make her give him—which so far hadn't been a dime—was for her to be dead. He asked the man why he was here.

"The murder of William. We've been informed of some new evidence, as I said, and you'd not believe how helpful it's been." He wondered if Benson had ratted him out, and remembered that the kid had no idea where he'd hidden the things that would point right to him in the death of Will. There were a great many little hidey holes all over the mountainside that he'd put things in. "We found the car that hit him too."

He looked at the man. There was no fucking way he'd found the car. Blake had made sure that no one would ever find it, and tried to think how he could learn what the man knew without giving himself away. Blake cleared his throat, trying to buy himself some time.

"I thought, back then, that no one had come forward about poor Will's death. I know there was something in the paper, and my sister, she never mentioned it either. They did ask me quite a few questions if I remember, but I wasn't in the area at the time. As I'm sure you already know." The man nodded. "I don't think I caught your name."

145

"I work for the FBI, James Whitlow." Blake asked him why the FBI was looking into an old murder. "Well, we were called in as a favor for someone. You'd be surprised how quick things can get moving when the president wants it looked into."

"The president of what?" He just looked at him and Blake felt foolish. "You don't have to tell me, but I thought it would be nice to know who would drag up a murder after all this time."

"The president of the United States. You know, President Howard Wayneright." Blake shook his head. "Yes, sir. Called me right up when Browning called and said she had found something. And when she finds something, you can bet that it's good information. She said that she and her sister-in-law were walking over the mountain, looking for the perfect tree, and found a cave. Found the car sitting right there in it like it had been waiting on them."

"Browning?" Agent Whitlow explained who she was. "Sister-in-law to my niece. Who just happened to be out walking around and found a cave. Do you have any idea how farfetched that sounds? There must be a thousand caves up there in that mountainside. How on earth did they find that one?"

"I don't rightly know myself, but you can ask her should you want. I'd be real nice about it with her this time if I was you. She's still a might pissed off at you for making them late for lunch." Blake felt sweat roll down his back and into his underwear. "Anyway, they were taking this walk while looking for the perfect tree when they ventured into a cave. Don't know why, but it was very helpful that they did, don't you think?"

No, he didn't fucking think it was helpful at all. When he'd pulled the car into that cave all those years ago, he'd

146

never thought of fingerprints or DNA. Hell, he wasn't even sure that there had been such evidence being collected then. In all this time, not once had he ever thought that anyone would go looking for the car, nor had he gone back to try and clean it up after things like computer analysis or testing came to light. Blake felt his heart pound harder in his chest when he thought of all the shit they might have already found up there.

"You have some questions for me about this?" He needed to get the man out of here and go to the mountain to see what they'd found. And he needed to get out of town fast if they really had found the car. Christ, this was really fucked up.

"Where were you the night he was killed, for starters? And if you can remember, why Will was working so late?" Blake wanted to tell him that he'd been running him down because Will had found out that Blake had been taking money out of his grandfather's checking account, but didn't think that would go over well. "In the event you don't know, it was April 8."

"I'll have to think on that. It was a long time ago, as I said." Whitlow just nodded, his notebook out in front of him and his pen poised. "I remember my sister was pregnant with her youngest and they were living with my grandfather. He never could hold down a job...I think that was the reason. But Will had been working the store that night and never arrived home. I think it broke her heart when he was killed."

"That's the story. And Will was a good worker by all accounts, and had given up a good job to come where his wife needed him to be. Nice man if you ask me. But where were you? We've accounted for everyone else that night. Of course, Brooklynn's story can't be confirmed by her, as you know."

He did know. She had died before he could kill her too.

The two of them, Will and Brooklynn, had threatened to

call the police on him. But when Will had turned up dead, she died before he could make good on killing her as well. And he figured that she'd gone on to be with her Will without telling his grandda or the police. Had she, he would have been in jail, even to this day, for what he'd done. Because as surely as he'd been stealing, they would have put two and two together in Will's death.

"I was on the farm." Whitlow shook his head. "Yes, I think I was. You could ask my grandda, but he's sadly no longer with us."

"There were other people there that night when the police went up there to tell Brooklynn that her husband had been murdered. They all said you weren't there. Something about an errand you'd had to rush out and do." He asked him who. "Well, there was Morgan Boyer, the retired banker. Also, his wife, Pauline, and their oldest two boys, Mike and David. I've got a list of names that I'm going to talk to about it, just to put all my ducks in a row, but they all had the same story. You left about two and didn't return for several days after."

"I don't remember who...what do you mean, retired? Boyer has been running the local bank for years. He's the one that.... Never mind. When did this happen?" He told him. "What the fuck is wrong with everyone that they're just doing as they fucking please? Brooke is off getting married. The banker is retiring. Have you looked into the bank to see if he's been stealing from it? Or are you just interested in harassing me?"

"Don't know what you mean about that, Blake. Morgan has been set to retire for the last few months. His replacement came in just a week ago and he's made the final push to leave. As for the wedding between Darcy and Brooke, well I'm thinking that wasn't as long in coming, but then, I guess they just loved each other and decided to tie things up." He said that

148

Brooke told him she would never marry. "Well, apparently she changed her mind. But back to this night in question, where were you?"

"I don't remember. Christ, it was twenty some years ago." He again told him twenty-six. "Twenty-six or fifty, I still don't know where I was."

"Did you have a grudge against Will? And before you answer that, you should know that we have witnesses that say you and he fought about money the day before he was killed. And most of the people that were around back then, they said that it was seldom when you two were together that you didn't call him names and threaten him. Bad timing that, threatening a man then him ending up dead." Blake closed his eyes, trying to figure out why all this was coming out now. "And Morgan said that you were behind in your house payments as well as taxes at the time. He said that you and he had words that morning too, about them. You were on the verge of losing everything. I guess you did later, didn't you?"

"I did manage to get that cleared up." Whitlow said that he'd not, his grandfather had. "So? It was caught up. What difference does it make who did it? He was a good man who did things for me. And you make it sound like I just got foreclosed on my home. I sold it, as a matter of fact."

"No, that's not right again. You signed it over to your grandfather when you went to prison the first time. And as far as him being a nice man and doing things for you…that was not all the time, was it? In fact, in the last few years he'd refused to pay any of your debts, hadn't he?" Blake got up to pace. This was not good, not good at all. How the hell had they found out all this? It had to be Brooke. She was doing this to him. "You've had your car repossessed in the last few weeks, you've been turned out of apartment after apartment. Even this one soon, I'm to understand. And I believe as of this morning that cell phone of yours doesn't work anymore. Nonpayment of the bill. You sure have sunk low, haven't you there, Blake?"

"Brooke won't give me any money." Whitlow asked why she'd have to do that. "Because she got my share of the money that Grandda had. I should have gotten most of it, and then the rest be divided up between the three of them. But she took it all. And now I'm out in the cold. Is that any way for someone to treat their uncle? Her having it all and not sharing with me, or even her own brother? There should be laws about that. Not leaving anything to your family when you have so much to leave behind."

"I think there is, as a matter of fact, but it won't do you diddly squat. The will states that you got yours and then some before Daniel died. And that he felt that he'd given you more than your fair share while he was living. Isn't that right, Blake?" Blake said nothing, but went to the refrigerator and pulled out a beer. Draining the bottle, he tossed the empty into the sink and tried to think. "You ever think where you were that night?"

"No...for Christ's sake, no. I have no idea where I was. For all I know I could have been sitting right next to him when he was hit." Whitlow stood up and told him he wasn't next to him, he knew that. "Then if you know so fucking much, tell me where I was, why don't you?"

Blake regretted the question almost as soon as it left his mouth. Something made Blake think that Whitlow knew where he'd been. The car. It was the fucking car that was going to get him caught. When he asked Whitlow if he had anything else for him, he told him no. Blake told him that he'd like for him to leave then.

"So you know, I'm coming back to finish this up. You

think on where you were really hard, and perhaps we can get things into perspective. Also, just in case you weren't aware of it, there is no statute of limitation on murder." And with that, he left.

Blake paced the living room for several minutes after the door closed behind the FBI agent. They had the car. But all he could think about was how deeply he'd put it in that cave. How much care he'd taken in making sure that there weren't any tire marks to lead the police there. Not that they'd ever looked on the mountain for it, but he'd gone back over the area several times as the search for the murderer went on, and there had been nothing. All along they'd been working on the theory that it had been a tourist and that they might never catch them. Blake had liked that idea very much.

He and Will had not liked each other...nearly anyone that came in contact with either of them knew that. The man wasn't good enough for the Rickson family as far as Blake was concerned. Will had been born poor, and he'd died that way too as far as Blake knew. And the fact that Brooklynn had never taken his name had only made Blake stronger in his conviction that Brooklynn had only married him to get back at Blake. He remembered the argument that had begun before the doors to the shop had been closed, and went on well after Blake had left Will there.

"No, that's not right. She has her own career and it would confuse people if she changed her name. It's on the marriage license as Rickson, and that's the way we want it." Blake had tried that night to piss off Will, enough that he'd have to shoot him. But the man had been calm and steady as ever. That was another reason that Blake had hated him. "Besides, Blake, what concern is it of yours how we live our life? It's not like you come around all that much. But you're not going to be getting any more money from Grandda's accounts. I've made sure of that."

"What did you do? Go and tell on me. Christ, he's my grandfather and nothing to you. Are you afraid that he won't like you? I got news for you, Will, he doesn't like you. He thinks you're lazy and stupid." Will only shook his head and said nothing. "Did you hear me? He doesn't like you."

"No, I think he loves me. As much as he does Brooklynn and the children. And he'll go on loving them well after you're in prison again, I think."

Nothing upset him. No matter how many times Blake tried to get him angry, all he did was walk away. The fucker had done it so much that night Blake had felt his temper just snap. All he'd wanted to do was go to the shop to get some cash and take a few more pieces of the pottery to sell, but Will was there waiting for him. As if he knew that he'd be coming by.

"There's nothing here for you, Blake. And we have all the proof we need to go to Daniel to let him know that you've been stealing from his account too." Blake asked him what he thought Grandda was going to do. "Nothing, it's already been done. The password has been changed on the account, so the ATM card you have is no longer valid. Also, the bank is going to ban you from using the account with any checks you have stolen, as well as all the clerks have your picture for when you try it that way. Brooklynn also had them cancel your credit cards, all of them you have around town. There won't be any more taking without his permission."

"You will change it all back right now, or so help me I'll make you live to regret fucking with me, Will. What did you think you were going to get out of this, anyway? You want it all for yourself, is that it? Or do you plan to live with him the rest of your life and then take it all when he's finally dead? I got news for you, Will...as his oldest grandchild, I'm going to get most of it. Brooklynn will get a little, but I'll have the bulk of the estate."

"If you say so. But I have a feeling that he's going to be around a lot longer than you think, and not give you another dime." He'd been right about that, Blake realized then. "And when we're finished talking to him about what we've learned, you'll be out all the sooner."

Blake had left then. His temper was hot, but he knew that beating up Will right now would only get him arrested. So he had gotten in his new car and sat there waiting for him to come out of the shop. Will had no doubt made sure that Brooklynn knew that they'd talked too, making him out to be the bad guy. It had been another hour and by then, Blake was so angry that he couldn't see straight.

When he saw Will moving down to the parking area behind the shop, he heard him singing, some old tune that his grandda sang when he was in the shed. Starting up his car, he pressed the gas pedal as hard as he could to the floorboard and drove right at him. Will turned at the last minute, and Blake had never forgotten what his face looked like when he realized that it was Blake that was killing him.

Blake had never enjoyed killing anyone as much as he had Will. And when he was down and depressed, like he was now, thinking of him flying up over the hood of the car and landing in the road behind him made Blake smile a little.

153

CHAPTER 10

Brooke didn't know what to say. The box, an old cigar box, had been handed to her by Bri a few moments ago, and she'd opened it thinking it was another joke gift. The Harrison men seemed to give those to each other a great deal.

"I wanted to give that to you, but I got called away." She nodded at Darcy. "Your grandda had it hidden away in Serendipity for the last twenty years. Pauline said that he had her looking for it and she held it for you. Do you like these things?"

"I have pictures of her wearing some of these things. She wore this on her wedding day to my dad." He pulled the long locket out and opened it up for her. It was almost exactly like the one that Darcy had given his mom not moments ago. When it was handed back to her, she touched her fingers to the couple there. On one side of the locket was her dad, the other her mom. "She was very beautiful, wasn't she?"

"Yes, she was. Very much so. And you look a great deal like her." Brooke looked at Darcy then. "I forgot when I got this that you'd not remember her. From what I've heard about her and her work, she was as famous as you and your grandda, and she was happy with your dad. Nikki and Storm are seeing if they can find any of her work out there and are letting me know. I'd like to have a couple of her works here, wouldn't you?"

"Yes, I'd like that very much. Grandda told me stories about them when I was older. He told me that he'd never seen a couple more in love than the two of them." He kissed her on the cheek. "I love you, Darcy. With all my heart."

"And I you, love." He kissed her then, putting another box on her lap. "This one I didn't really find for you. I actually had help from your grandfather. And so you know, I wanted to get you a ring, but Dad told me about how you can't wear them around a kiln."

When she began to peel the paper off the little box, she told him about the one time she'd worn an underwire bra while unloading a kiln. "It was still pretty hot, about two hundred to two-fifty. I leaned in to take out the first piece and felt this stabbing pain in my chest. I thought I'd landed on a kiln pin. So I moved. Reaching in again, I sat up so quickly — it was hotter, you see, having had time to warm more — that I knocked myself into the wall behind me. The wires in my bra had burnt my tender skin so badly that I couldn't wear a bra for a week after that."

"I bet your grandda got a kick out of that." She said that he'd laughed himself right off the chair he'd been sitting on. "I can almost see it now. Were you hurt badly?"

"Mostly my pride. But I didn't ever wear any kind of wiring again when I opened a kiln. Christ, I had a blister all along the underside of each boob for a week." She opened the box and looked at the wrist watch laying in the pretty box. "Oh Darcy. It's beautiful."

And it was. The watch was old; she'd bet anything that it was at least fifty years old or more. Picking it up out of the velvet, he told her how he'd come to have it for her. And for her to read the back of it.

"*With all my heart, I love you.*" There was nothing else, and she knew that whoever had put it there had done so with their own hand. The writing was off just a little, yet it meant more to her than she could have thought.

"We thought, Pauline and I, that it belonged to your mom. It was in the little box of things that came with the combs and other things. But the guy who fixed it and cleaned it up for me said that it might have been worn by her, but it was actually your great grandmother's. I guess he'd repaired it once when she'd broken the clasp on it. Your grandda—he's the one that wrote on the back—never said much about it, but he knew that he'd purchased it for her from a mail-order catalog." He helped her put the watch on and it fit. "Those are diamonds around the face, and the four gems that mark noon, three, six, and nine are emerald, ruby, topaz, and sapphire respectively."

"I never saw this. Not that I remember." He held her to him and she snuggled up under his chin, watching the others open gifts. She had hers for Darcy behind her back, one that she hoped with all her heart he'd like. It was her grandda's pocket watch that she'd had cleaned just for him. When Mac picked up the one she'd given him, she felt her body tense up. This was something she'd not been sure of.

Mac looked at her when he took the poster out of the box. He looked thrilled with it, and it wasn't even the gift. When he kissed her on the cheek and thanked her for it, Brooke laughed.

"That's not the gift, goofy." He told her that it was perfect, that he'd have it framed and put in his new pottery collection room. "What I mean is, that's not what we got you. It's the piece. I'm giving you the piece."

"No." She nodded. "Oh no, that's too.... I mean, don't get me wrong, I want it, but it's too much. I saw this, but it's too much."

"It would mean a great deal to me if you were to take it, please. You're sort of responsible for bringing us together. You and Nikki. I've given all of your family a piece of my work, but this is my grandfather's." He sat down, staring at the poster with the strangest look on his face. "If you don't care for it, you can go and find one that you—"

"It's not that. I'm just so touched by this. Waterfall...it's called Waterfall, isn't it?" She nodded. "The only piece that he made that was stacked like your work. When I saw it in the gallery, I remember thinking that I could feel the water spilling over it, the trees were so alive. You have no idea how you've made me feel by trusting me with a piece of his life."

"You're very welcome." He stood up and grinned at her. She wasn't sure that she liked that look at all. "What is it?"

"We found something for you. All of us. Nikki got on this kick after she talked to Darcy, and we searched for a week. Then, all of a sudden, I remembered where I had seen it. Right in my own town." She asked him what he was talking about. "Here, open this. It's from us, but a very good friend said you should have it."

She took the envelope with trembling hands. Looking at Darcy was no help...he looked as confused as she felt. When the picture fell out in her lap, she could only stare at it. It was the very first piece she'd sold.

"Mason, he's been a friend of ours since Storm came into our family. He said that he'd like to talk to you. But he's a vampire, and you'd have to invite him in." Standing up, she asked him if he was near. "Yes. He's been here for a few days helping out with your uncle."

Going with the family, she opened the front door to find a tall, very young looking man. He smiled at her, not even bothering to hide his fangs. She wanted to hug him, but she had to gather her wits about her first.

"Would you like to come into our home and enjoy Christmas with us?" He nodded, but didn't move. "I'd very much like to thank you by giving you a hug for what you've given me. Did you know that I've been looking for this since I had my first showing?"

"I did not. However, I have had my eye on you for a long time." He looked behind her and she turned to see Darcy there. "It is his home as well, is it not?"

"Yes. It is. Everything I have is now his too." Mason winked at her and she knew that it was true. Everything, including herself, belonged to Darcy. And when he invited him in to join them as well, the big vampire stepped over the threshold and hugged them both.

They were seated around the big tree decorated with the most beautiful ornaments she'd ever seen. Brooke thought perhaps she might have them all here every holiday if they'd come. Not that she thought she'd have much trouble convincing them of that. When Mason asked to speak to her, she moved over on the couch to make room. When he sat, all prim and proper, she knew that she could really like this man.

"I'm a blunt man. Years of living has given me no patience for beating around bushes to see where I land. I've been to see your brother, Benson. He is...I was going to say that he is not well, but that would be an understatement. Did you know that he uses drugs?" She said that she did, that was one of the reasons she knew that he stole from her. "It is. But in his drug usage, he has picked up something, a virus that is killing him. I'm afraid that he is not long for this world."

"He's that sick?" He nodded his head and she had to think, and knew what it might be. "He's going to end his life then. He's tried before, but I think it was only to gain some attention from us."

"It was. I have.... As an old vampire, I have abilities that have given me some insight into a person's mind. Not only can I read their thoughts and desires, but I can see the darkness that is there as well, and manipulate a mind should I need to. I have not done anything to your brother, so you know. I did think for a moment to try and change his mind. But I believe, in this, it might be easier on him should he do things his way." Brooke nodded, not really sure how she felt about it. "He has been ill for some time, Brooke, too long for anyone to help him now."

"Does my uncle know?" He said that he did. "And he has known for some time, I'm betting. He did nothing to help him, did he?"

"I don't think he wanted him to live any more than he does you." Brooke nodded. "I have something else to tell you. Your uncle, we think he might have killed your father. And in turn, your mother as well. I'm sorry to tell you this today, but it is important that you keep safe. He'll come for you now, today, if the things we have put into motion are fruitful."

"Grandda told me he thought Uncle Blake had killed my father. I think that was the main reason that he never trusted him very much." Mason leaned back on the couch, but it occurred to her that he was still very aware of things going on even though he looked relaxed. "There was never any proof, of course. Things like outside cameras and cell phones to track him with weren't around then. And if they were, I doubt that we would have had them. But Uncle Blake hated my dad, he told me that much. Uncle Blake never has good things to say about my dad, or my mom for that matter."

"Storm has some good connections, and she sent a man to see your uncle yesterday. She knew that the car that had hit your father had to be somewhere on this property, but.... Well, you know this mountain better than most, and I would bet you don't even know of all the hiding places that it could have been in." She asked him if he meant a cave. "We do. James gave your uncle the impression that he worked as an agent, when all he does for the agency is clean the windows. After a few lessons on what to say, I think he was able to get your uncle in enough of a panic mode to have him go and see if the car was actually found. We're hoping, and we believe, that he will lead them to the car."

"So this James person, he told him something like you'd found the car, and what? You had questions for him about it?" Mason nodded. "And if he didn't do it, and I'm not saying that he didn't, do you think he's...? Never mind. He is just stupid enough to go and see what you've been able to find on it. And Benson, did he know about the car as well?"

"No. He thinks that his uncle killed his dad, or had him killed. But he knows nothing of the car or where it might be. He thinks, as a great many people did at the time, that the murderer either put it into one of the deep lakes higher on the mountains, or it was driven off by an unsuspecting tourist after it was stolen, used, and then returned."

Brooke tried to digest this and thought of all the times she'd heard her uncle claim that her dad was nothing but a money hungry fool who had gotten himself killed because he had married outside his circle.

"The car is a Ford, two door, and dark blue." Mason asked her how she knew this. "Grandda had some paperwork in the pottery room. Some of it was a title for a car in my uncle's name. He asked him about it once—it seemed so casual at the time—but Uncle Blake went nuts. Told my grandda that he should mind his own business before he ended up as dead as his precious Brooklynn. It was just after he asked him about it that money was cut off, and Grandda didn't pay any more families when Blake did something to them. That was right after Uncle Blake ended up in prison the first time."

Mason stood up and held out his hand to her. She took it before she could think that it might not be such a good idea. She found herself suddenly in a dark cave standing next to a car. A blue Ford two door sedan. She didn't even panic when she realized where she was. Looking at Mason, she knew for some reason that he'd not brought her here to hurt her.

"I'm going to go and get Storm and Darcy. Don't leave here, Brooke." She nodded. "Blake is on his way here, just about a hundred yards away. And he's armed. Please do not go out and confront him."

"I won't. I don't want to be hurt either." He nodded, then disappeared.

Moving to the front of the car, she started to rub her hand on the dust, but caught herself in time. Fingerprints, she thought; she didn't want her prints messing up his.

~~~

Blake didn't see anyone around, and there hadn't been anyone in the area for the several hours that he'd been there. He might have been there sooner but he'd gotten turned around, his landmarks no longer where he remembered them. But as soon as he saw the opening of the cave, he knew that he'd found it. And now he'd been watching it for two hours and not one person had come out or gone into it. Nor was there any tape around the place. Surely someone would have done that to keep strangers out.

Lied. That agent had lied to him. Blake had no idea why he knew that...he just knew that he did. Or they had found another car in another cave and were asking him about it.

Christ, that would be funny. Another murderer using the same method of getting rid of the car.

"Only I've not been caught, as this guy apparently has." Blake started forward, just to check the place out, but heard something. He had a deathly fear of bears, and stood as still as he could possibly make himself. His knees were trembling a little too much, and he knew that a fucking bear was going to kill him. After a few more moments, he heard it again and realized someone was crying.

Moving to the cave again, he was careful where he stepped. Not that he thought his fucking niece would allow traps on the land, but people, dishonest people like himself, would do it for some extra cash. Trapping animals on this mountain had kept him in cash since he'd been a kid and had run into one of them with a fox in its jaws.

He heard the sound again when he was within a few feet of the opening. Concentrating on it, wanting to make sure that it wasn't some fucking animal and not an actual person boo-hooing, he took one too many steps forward.

The sound, the snapping of the jaws closing, was what told him he was in trouble. The pain, and there was a great deal of it, took him to the ground a few seconds later. The trap, old and rusty, was shut around his calf, bones and blood sticking out of it around his bloodied pant leg. Screaming now, uncaring of the person inside the cave hearing him, Blake knew that if he didn't get help soon, he'd be dead by morning.

"Merry fucking Christmas to me," he said out loud when no one came rushing out. He laid back on the ground, each movement making him sick to his stomach, until he leaned over and dry-heaved several times before he simply sat up. Christ, he hurt. And he'd not thought to bring anything with him when he'd left his place other than his fucking gun. Which was currently under his broken leg and blood, he only just remembered. "Will nothing ever fucking go right for me? Not even just one bloody time?"

Crying from the pain, he stared at the trap for several seconds before what had happened sunk in. He'd been caught by one of his own stupid traps. Blake wondered what the hell was wrong with the universe. Why was it forever conspiring against him?

His name, engraved on it, told whoever came across it that it belonged to him. And that touching it, or anything in it, meant death. It didn't actually say that, but the skull and crossbones under his name, crudely done, said it all. Blake started to lay back again, but the sound of his name had him looking in the direction of the cave.

"Hello, Uncle Blake. I see you've managed to get yourself trapped, haven't you? Have I mentioned lately how fucking stupid you are?" He stared at Brooke, wondering what it was about her that was so different. "Did you have to kill him?"

"Who?" He had a feeling that she meant her dad but wanted to be sure. He'd been killing people to get what he wanted for a very long time. "Perhaps you could narrow it down for me, Brooke darling. I've had a very profitable and long life, you know."

She sat on a stone not far from where he was. Blake couldn't touch her, not with this thing on his leg, but he might be able to kill her if he could get to his gun. But touching even the dirt under his broken and shattered bones caused him to cry out in pain.

"Not so profitable lately, is it? And are there so many that you can't put a finger on just who I might be talking about? My father. You killed him, didn't you?" Blake wondered for a moment if she was trying to get him to confess to something, but dismissed that. She was just too fucking stupid to try anything like that. And besides, who the hell was around to hear him? "Answer me, damn it."

"Yes. The fucker was in my way. Did you know that he and your mother were trying to get Grandda to cut me off even then? Christ, I had so much riding on Brooklynn dying in childbirth that killing off your father was just the next step in my plan. But she did something nice to me for a change, and died after whelping that fucking brat Brody. Where is he, by the way? He and I have some unfinished business."

"Like what? You want him dead too? Or is it because he knew what you and Benson were going to do with my body once you killed me?" He nodded without thinking. The pain was making itself known to the rest of his body, and he was going to be sick again. "I have news for you, Blake...you're not going to be able to hurt any of us again."

"You thinking of just leaving me out here? You won't make me believe that, Brooke. You're not only just like your mother, but you won't hurt a fucking bug much less leave me to rot here." He laughed, causing his leg to pain him more. "Get me some help, Brooke. I swear to Christ when I'm out of this, I'm going to go away for a long time."

"You are at that. The police know where the car is. Did you know that?" He told her that she lied. "Do I? Well, I guess we'll find out. I'm supposed to let them know when you show up. I guess I'm bait, you could say. I don't think they counted on you being caught like this, but I'm glad. It gives me the opportunity to ask you questions. And believe me, I have a few."

She tossed a cell phone just short of him being able to reach for it, then picked up a large stone and crushed it. He cried out...there wasn't any help coming for him through that thing.

165

"You're not nice, did I ever tell you that? And I've hated you all your fucking life. You and Grandda were a pair, I'll give you that. Working with your heads together like you knew some great secret and wasn't going to share it with the rest of us." He laughed then, costing him a great deal of painful reminders that he was still fucking trapped. "Grandda might have come around if you hadn't been going to him about every little thing I did to you. Fuck, Brooke, come here and help me out of this thing before I bleed to death."

"I hope you do." He stared at her. "You killed my father that night, then you hid the car in a cave on the very property you were to own."

"What are you talking about?"

She laughed and stood up. He thought for sure she was going to leave him there without answers, and he begged her to tell him.

"Didn't you know? Grandda had given you this part of the land before Mom died. This cave and nearly fifty acres of your own land to do with as you pleased. You could have even put those traps on it that you loved so much. But when he figured out that you'd killed Dad—yes, he knew it—he decided that he wasn't giving you any reason to be close to us. Not me nor my brothers. Then you started cultivating Benson to be your little soldier, and he'd had enough of both of you."

"You lie." She said that she had no reason to, he wasn't going to get to live there anyway. "Why didn't you tell me? Why didn't anyone tell me?"

"Perhaps no one figured you'd kill two people in the world that meant a lot to him." She paced the space in front of him. Christ, he was sick with pain and needed her to help him. "I'm not sure what you think is going to happen, Blake, but I'm not going to help you. I might have a few weeks ago, given you

166

enough to get a fresh start, but I'm done with you. Forever."

"So you're just going to leave me out here? For some animal to come along and kill me? Or was your plan to just watch me bleed to death?" He laughed. "That would make you a murderer, Brooke. And makes you no different than me."

"No, what it makes me is the person who brought you down." He looked to where she nodded. "I'd like you to meet some friends of mine. Along with my family, I'd like to introduce you to the people who have been recording every word that you said. Very nice of you to tell them everything that they needed." She turned and walked away from him.

"Come back here, you bitch. You can't do this to me. You hear me, come the fuck back here and tell them to let me go. Brooke?" He tried to move, to go after her, but a gun to the back of his head stopped him. "You gonna shoot me in cold blood?"

"I thought about it." He didn't recognize the woman's voice. "I actually thought, yeppers, I could kill him by just saying that my finger slipped. It worked for a friend of mine once. But I thought, nah, he'll have so much fun in prison. And that is where you're headed, by the way. Provided you make it down the mountain. Will you? I'd very much like for you not to, but who knows? You might do the world a favor and just keel over and die for us."

"You have no reason to kill me. I've done nothing wrong." She laughed. "Whatever I said, you have no proof of anything."

He heard a click, then something whined. When his own voice came back to him, loud and clear, he heard himself admit to not just killing his brother-in-law, but his plan to kill his sister as well. Blake knew then he was so fucked.

167

CHAPTER 11

The clay wasn't doing what she wanted it to. Every time she thought she had it right where she wanted it to go, it would bobble a little and she'd have to stop. Finally backing from the wheel, she just stared at the clay and thought about what had happened over the last few days.

Benson had killed himself two days after Christmas, leaving her uncle a note and telling him that he hoped that he killed her and her new husband. The bullet to his head had not done the job, and Benson had bled to death in a cheap hotel room all alone. His body had to be cremated and the room he'd been in had been quarantined, more than likely never to be used for anything other than maybe a storage area again.

Blake was in jail, and would be for a very long time. His trial, set for some time in April of next year, was going to be huge. Not only did they have the murder weapon that had killed her father, but Blake admitting to wanting to kill her mom as well had opened up a great many doors. Two people, people she didn't know, had come forth to say that they had worked with Blake on other murders as well as a string of robberies, including her home. He had asked to see her several times. She wasn't sure if she wanted to deal with him right now, if ever.

Brody was home. He'd come home yesterday and had

told her that he would stay for a little while. He and Darcy had gone down to the new store and were cleaning out the inventory that they weren't going to keep, as well as making a list of things that they might need. She'd never seen Brody so excited about something before. He had also sat down with her and they talked.

"I'm not going to go and see Blake, ever." She told him she understood. "No, you can't. No one does. He.... I never told anyone this, but he tried to kill me once. When I was ten. He'd hired some guy to run me down after school."

"What did you do? Why didn't you tell anyone?" He told her that he'd been too afraid. "It's why you never stayed around here much, isn't it? You didn't want to be hurt by him anymore. Oh Brody, I wish I would have known. I could have helped you."

"Like you did yourself." She wasn't sure what he knew and he laughed a little. "He beat you whenever he could, we both know that. And had Grandda known what he did to you before he died, I'm sure that being sick or not, he would have killed him."

"Blake drugged me. I had no way of knowing where I was." He nodded. "I just woke up in a dark place and nearly fell down a cavern when I tried to make my way out. I was so afraid that I'd die in there and no one would find me."

"But you made it out and never said a word to anyone." She nodded. "Did you tell the police about it after he was taken into custody? Or Darcy? He'd be pretty pissed, I bet."

"He knows. I told him last night. I still have nightmares about it, and I woke screaming." Brooke and Brody had been so hurt by two people that they could have loved so very much. She'd asked him what he was going to do now.

"Live. Try to live without fear and thinking that someone

is out to hurt me or talk badly about me. Grandda had me seeing someone long ago and I stopped. I was thinking I'd go back, see if I can get a better grip on my life and what I feel all the time." She started to cry. "Don't, Brooke, please. None of this is our fault. We did the best we could with what we had. Grandda knew we were hurting and did his best to protect us, but he could only do so much."

"I miss him so very much." Brody had told her that he did as well. "We have each other now. Right? And when we get to feeling lost or whatever, we know that we can depend on ourselves."

"You have Darcy now. And believe it or not, I have as well. He's a very good man. I hope you know that." She had told him she did. "Good. Now, I'm going to bed and not lock the door. Well, I might not lock the door. Oh, who am I kidding, I'm locking it. I love you, Running Water."

"And I love you, Shadow of Man."

Now she stood here all alone, with not a clue of what she'd been thinking in getting married to a man she barely knew. Taking deep breaths and letting them out slowly, she looked up when someone said her name. Morgan was standing just on the other side of the wheel from her. She'd not even heard him come in.

"There are many things I could say to you now." She nodded. "But I will not. You would only tell me to fuck off or something like that, and I'd laugh. Which I believe would make you more upset."

"I'm all alone." He asked her how she thought that. "I don't have anyone left in my family. Brody is going to leave me again, Darcy is going to realize that I'm not very easy to get along with and that I like to be by myself. What sort of mate am I that enjoys my own company over others? And you're moving away."

"I am. To a city not far from here. Not walking distance, mind you, but close enough for you to call me to you." She said nothing. "Brody will know that you will forever welcome him here with open arms. That he will have a home here, a place to rest his worn body, and love in you. The two of you might be at a distance, but you are far from apart."

"And Darcy? What is it about him that you can give me advice on?" He told her none. "So you believe that he will leave me."

"No, I did not say that. But you know the answer to your unfounded fears as well as I. Why would he leave you? He loves you more than he does his own life. Will he tire of you? I cannot imagine why he would. I have known you since before you were born and I have not tired of you." He sat in the chair before continuing. "As for your liking to be alone, I think he understands that more than you do at times. You are a creative person, a woman who uses her mind as well as her body to create. And when you are thinking, as you are too much at the moment, you need space to do so. I think that he is a person that will give you what you need when you need it, whether it be the space you think you need or holding you when you need that as well."

"He's my husband." Morgan said that he was well aware of that, he'd married them. "I don't know how to be a wife."

"You are now grasping at straws, Running Water. Do you know how to love him? To keep him as safe as you can?" She said that she did. "And do you think he frets over the fact that you are working out here and not cooking him meals, cleaning the house, making the bed?"

"He does all of that. And he seems to enjoy it." Morgan nodded. "What if he decides that he doesn't want to do that anymore? Then what?"

"Then you hire someone to come and do it for you. It is not as if either of you could not afford it. I think I heard that Dark One has more money than even you do, and I thought you to have it all." She laughed when he did. Brooke asked him why Dark One for Darcy. "It is the meaning of his name, the same as you are Running Water. But I think that he is a dark horse as well, one that will not sit by and do nothing while you are working. He will pull his weight and more, I think. I have also heard that he is still working for his family, and has a business here as well as one in his hometown. Not a man that sounds like he would tire of things easily."

"We've set up an office for him to work from here, as well as a storefront in town. Harrison Enterprise has expanded nicely in this area, and he's hired two people to work for him too." Morgan said he knew both and that they were a part of his son's new pack. The clay called to her and she leaned over it to bring it to life as she talked to Morgan. "I have a gallery showing in three months. I'm going to go as Brooke Rickson Harrison this time."

"Good for you. Your parents and grandfather would be very proud of you."

Forming the clay into the shape she could see in her head, she lost herself for several moments. Morgan said something, but the clay was speaking louder and she listened.

When she lifted her head he was gone, and the bottle of water that she'd been drinking when he'd arrived was warm. Looking at the clock across the room, she realized how incredibly late it was. She'd been out here for nearly six hours.

And she'd been busy too.

There were nine large forms on the shelf next to her, and two more on the one that she'd moved away at some point.

They were going to be two pieces of art, pieces that she could see finished as she cleaned up her wheel and then her hands and arms. By the time she had the lights off and her pieces covered, Brooke felt good about her time out here. Walking to the house, she stopped to look at it.

Darcy was home; there were lights on in the front of the house, as well in the back where the kitchen was. Music was playing somewhere...classical like they both enjoyed. Brooke could smell the charcoal heating up, and knew that they'd be having steaks on the grill. When she got a whiff of something sweet too, Brooke grinned. Andi had left behind a freezer shelf of pies and cakes before they all left this morning, and something was baking.

Opening the door to the kitchen, she watched him as he talked to someone, using the hands free set he'd gotten for Christmas as he cut out biscuits. When he saw her, he winked but continued to talk for several more minutes. She got some tea and sat down to wait.

~~~

Darcy wanted to hang up on the client and kiss his wife, but knew that he'd only call back again. The man was having a crisis and he wanted Darcy to fix it yesterday. Waiting for a break in his never ending complaints about how his business was failing, Darcy kissed Brooke on the mouth and asked her quietly if she was ready to eat.

"Yes. What can I do?" He told her he had it under control and paused when Mr. White asked him if he'd come out to help him.

"I've told you, several times already, that I'd be out on Monday. I'm not going to travel out there to help you over a holiday weekend. You said yourself that the business was closed until then. And coming out now would only make me

174

have to wait to see where your issues are. I'll be there Monday afternoon, as we discussed last week." The man whined again about how he was losing money every day. "Yes you are. A great deal of it, but I can't figure anything out until I get there on Monday like we planned."

"I heard you and your company are the best. I need the best working on this now." Darcy said nothing as he put the biscuits, something that he was trying to make as well as Andi, into the hot oven. "I'll double what you're asking if you can fix this for me."

He wanted to tell him he wasn't going to come out. To tell the man that he had a new wife and home that he'd rather be in. And not halfway across the United States with him. Instead, he told him that he'd see him on Monday and hung up. There was only so much he could do over the phone, and he wasn't going to hold his hand long distance.

"I've gotten a lot done, how about you?" She told him about the pieces that she'd thrown and how she could see the finished product. "I think the way your mind works is amazing. I can see what is wrong in a business pretty quickly, but not the end result without hours of going over everything. You must love it when it turns out the way you saw it."

"Sometimes it does what it's supposed to, most of the time really, but not always. A piece can break in the set and then I'm not sure what to do with it." She took a cracker with cheese on it when he offered. "How much more do you have to do in the store? I'm betting it's a mess."

"It is. Pauline had so much inventory in the back I'm thinking of having a huge sale just to get rid of a lot of it. There are boxes of tissue paper back there that have a ship date from six years ago. I think she must have gotten a pretty good deal on it, because there are nineteen boxes with the same date."

They both laughed. "Anyway, Brody found some boxes of toys in the basement. Which, I might add, I never went down to. He said he'd take care of it for me. I hate basements."

"I hate dark areas too." He'd forgotten about her brush in the cave, but she changed the subject before he could tell her he was sorry for bringing it up. "Mac called me. His piece arrived. I think he's more excited about that than he is the new baby. Not really, but he thanked me like fifty times for it."

"My dad called me when I was at the shop too. His and Mom's gift arrived in the same shipment." She flushed and he had to smile. "I don't think they expected you to give them the house in town so that they could have a place to stay when they came here."

"Well, when we told them that they could all come back anytime they wanted, your mom made a fuss about not wanting to intrude on us. I think it's silly, especially when we have this big house, but I had hoped that it would make them feel like they'd not have to wait to be invited to come down." She laughed a little as she continued. "Did your dad happen to mention the lake in the back of the property? I've never seen a man so obsessed with drowning worms, as he calls it."

"Yes, he did. Several times."

Darcy looked at the phone when it rang again. It was White. So instead of answering it again and getting wrapped up in the man's trouble, he picked up the platter with the steaks on it and went out to the deck to grill. He was glad when Brooke came out to join him.

"I'd like for you to change me." He nearly dropped the fork he'd brought out to flip the steaks with. "Not now, but as soon as the show in April is over. I have to go to that. Well, I don't have to, but I want to. And they want sixty pieces. I have them, but I need to finish the.... I'm babbling. I don't want you to tell me no, I guess."

"I wasn't going to." He looked out at their yard. It wasn't really a yard so much as a forest, with caves and wild animals that would kill without hesitation. "We'd encounter animals here that I've never been around before. Not that I'm saying that I'm not excited about the prospect of it, but it's a little scary as well."

"Will you stand perfectly still for a moment?" He told her he would. And when she put her fingers in her mouth and whistled, he was both impressed and jealous. He could barely whistle at all, much less make a sound like that. "Look at them. They're natural to this area."

The red fox family with their kits came almost to the deck where they were. The male watched him carefully as his children came right up on the deck and took the small treats that Brooke was handing out. When he looked at the tree line again, there were three bears, big black ones, that roared but kept their distance until she stepped down on the ground. He started to caution her but she spoke low to him.

"The bears won't come any closer than where they are now. The cubs, when they have them, will come closer sometimes, but not often. I think they're being respectful or something. The fox have been coming here for years. My grandda first started feeding them when the winter was bad and they came to see him." He saw the deer then, about a dozen of them, come from the opposite direction the bears were at, and with them were two elk. They were huge from a distance, but this close, they were fucking scary. "There are some wild wolves and a few coyotes as well, but they don't come out too often in the daylight. I think Morgan has a deal with them, because they leave the animals that come close to the house alone."

"You have your own little farm here." She laughed a

little, and one of the kits came up to where he was standing. Not moving quickly, he dropped one of the treats from the container she'd opened down to him. The other two kits joined their brother for their own treats after that.

When she sat on the deck steps, he moved to join her. The bears came and went in and out of the woods, the elk grazed closer to the barn but not the house, and the deer seemed to not care about anything, and nearly joined them on the deck. When the steaks were done, he got up to see to them, and wasn't surprised to see that all the animals had gone back to their dens. Going inside, he thought about changing Brooke and agreed it was a great idea.

Darcy took care of the cleanup while she did the laundry. When they were finished, instead of going to watch some television as he normally would have, they sat on the couch and read books. There was something so purely laid back about it that he decided that he was never buying a television for the house, and that when he got his things from home, he was going to see about getting the turntable. It was old and probably needed to be cleaned, but he was going to get it set up so they could listen to real music and not anything canned or from a station. Darcy really liked the quiet life.

CHAPTER 12

"Liam, can you come out here?" Liam frowned when he picked up his calendar to see when he had a clear few days, and told Darcy that he couldn't come out until Wednesday. This was only Thursday of the week before. "Good, that should help a great deal. I'm here at White's Toys, and things are.... I don't know what to do, to be honest."

"What is going on? I mean, do you need me to come out now? Is it something to do with Brooke?" He assured him it was the business, not his personal life. "I heard from Riordan that there was something going on out there. And you told me before you left that the man was driving you crazy with constant calls."

"He has this son. You remember about four or five years ago when that business owner's son was stealing the product from the trucks before they left the lot?" He said that he did. "Well, it's something like that, but I can't put my finger on it. It's not the son, I don't think. He's the one telling me that is the problem. Nothing is missing on the trucks. Not when they leave here, nor when they arrive at the destination. But the inventory is all fucked up."

"That is weird. Have you looked into the orders? I mean, are they being messed with?" He told him that he had a call into three of the shops where things had gone over the last

179

week, and no one was calling him back. "Give me the names and I'll see what I can do here."

After giving him all that he had, Darcy sighed heavily. "Liam, the warehouse is short over sixty million in inventory. Yet the invoices are all correct as far as I can tell, and they match up with the orders that are sent to be filled. And they run a really tight ship here. At least within the building. Everyone is scanned and checked for inventory before they leave for the day, and they count and recount each truck when it comes. I don't get it."

Neither did he. Christ, sixty million? Where the fuck was it? He told Darcy that he'd call him as soon as he had something. As soon as he hung up, he called the first of the shops. The manager wasn't in to talk to him. And when he asked when he would be in to do so, he was hung up on. He thought of calling back, but dialed the next number on the list from Darcy.

"This is Harrison Enterprise. We're doing a spot check on your inventory from White's Toys. Can you answer a few questions for me?" He heard the phone being put down and started to hang up when he heard someone talking. He listened carefully, taking notes on names and information that he could get.

"It's that company again." A second person asked what company. "Harrison something. They want to talk to someone about inventory."

"Christ, don't they have enough shit going on without bothering me? Tell him that we're not going to be ordering from Whites again, not in any lifetimes. Never mind. I will." He heard the phone being put on hold, then some music. He was prepared to ask as much as he could before the other person spoke when the phone was picked up. "This is Betty Keith. Please don't call here again. I have had it up to my ass with White and his fucking toys that don't work half the time and are broken the other half. I've spent more time in trying to get replacements and refunds on this than I think is necessary. When I can get either. If you want to know what the hell is going on, then welcome to my world. I'm too busy and too tired to fuck with it anymore."

"We're trying to figure out what is going on at the warehouse." She snorted at him. "My company, who is only affiliated with White's to see whether we can save his company or not, has nothing to do with the product he sends out."

"Neither does he, I don't think. The last shipment that came in should have been ninety-four boxes. Not a huge order by any means, but I was giving them one more try to see if we could resolve this. But when the order got here, not only was it less than we wanted, but when I called to ask about it, I was told that was the order I'd sent in. The woman on the phone assured me that she had it right in front of her, and I'd ordered just fifty cases." He asked her how she ordered, by phone or fax. "Online. I can do that after hours and not be bothered by sales pitches. But lately that's been messed up as well. My husband and I are trying to run a nice little business here, and this is not helping us."

"No, I would imagine it isn't. You mentioned broken and unusable toys. Can you tell me about a few of those? I'm trying to fix this for you and them." The woman sounded resigned to the fact that she wasn't going to get anything from him or the company. "I'll make sure that you're given a full refund."

"I've heard that before. Three times now. And the total amount of what they owe me now is more than I made all of last month. And even though it's their mistake, they're making me pay for return shipping. Do you have any idea how much that costs? That is no way to run a business." He told her that he was sorry. "Yeah, so am I."

He wrote down everything she told him; how the products sometimes didn't match what was on the box...not the case, but the toy boxes themselves; how batteries included usually meant that they were either dead when they got there or corroded too badly to use; and how there were mouse droppings in some of the boxes.

"Mouse droppings?" She assured him that she'd grown up on a farm, and knew mouse shit when she saw it. "I understand. And what does the company say when you tell them about this? I'm assuming that it's not much."

"Oh, they have plenty to say. Like I should call someone in to take care of it, that there is no way they have that on their end. Also that if the boxes don't match the toys, there is little that they can do about that. It wasn't their fault. Wasn't their fault? How the hell is that even possible? Christ, it's like working with a five-year-old when I have to call in there to complain. I just decided that even though they used to be a good company with quality things, I'm not going to be dealing with them anymore. And the money that they owe me isn't ever coming, so I'm out that as well."

Liam hung up a few minutes later armed with enough information that he wasn't sure if he should call anyone else. But he did the next two on the list, and got basically the same information, only a little more colorful. The woman he'd talked to at Basic Fun had told him not only where he could stick his helping the White company, but that he could take Mr. White and his secretary with him. Ms. Wende had made more than one enemy of stores, it seemed. Liam called Darcy back and told him what he'd been able to find out.

"I've met Ms. Wende. She's a peach, and not the warm and fuzzy kind. More like the skin covers the pit kind of person."

Liam laughed. "I've tried to get inventory sheets from her, as well as outgoing truck information, and she just sits there filing her nails like that's all she does. Until Mr. White or his son comes around. Then it's all business with a capital B and she's all over them. Sickening. I told them about what I've run into, and all I get from them is that she's been there for a while and they've not had any trouble with her before this."

"Is she the one, you think? Causing the trouble?" Darcy told him that not only did she not have a computer at her desk, there didn't seem to be anything to take notes with. "You mean she's just a front?"

"I have no idea what her deal is. She answers the phone when it rings. No one asks her to file anything. And as I said, you can't get her to give you anything either." Liam said he'd look into her. "I tried, believe me I tried, but all I can get is that she's employed here."

"And that won't be for much longer the way things are going for the company. Their stock is down another five percent from yesterday." Liam started finishing up what he was doing. He'd go out today and see what he could do to help his brother on this. "I can be there by dinner. Can you swing a hotel for me?"

"I can do you one better. I'm staying in this really nice suite that has two bedrooms. If you don't mind, you can bunk with me." Liam liked that idea. "Good. We'll go over what you find and see what we can figure out. I'm going to try again to get some paperwork."

Liam hung up again and tried to think how to get any information. Going over the paperwork again, he found the name of an outside trucking company that occasionally did some short hops or turn arounds for them.

When a driver dropped off their load at a different

183

company, sometimes they would call around and ask if they had something going in their direction. It would be a way for them to get paid going home, and the company that used them would save money. There were two names on the list.

The first one was an independent, so he left them for later and called the second company. After getting the run around for ten minutes, he finally got to talk to someone in shipping. The man told him that they hadn't been hauling for White's for some time now. But he didn't know why.

"Is there any way you can find out?" He said that he could, but half his staff was out on sick leave. "I know that there is a lot of flu going around."

Liam had no idea if there was flu or not, but he figured that there was always something going around. It was winter after all. But when the man told him he'd call him back when he could find something, Liam gave him his cell number and thanked him. The second call went unanswered. But he did leave a message.

"I'm with Harrison Enterprise. I'm doing some checking on outbound loads you might have hauled for White's Toys. If you could give me a call back at my cell number, I'd really appreciate it." He gave the voice message his number and hung up.

Going home, he packed a bag and headed to the hangar. He had called ahead to have the jet ready, and before he could get settled, they were in the air. Ten minutes in, his cell went off. The independent driver was getting back to him.

~~~

Hudson wasn't sure why Harrison was calling her, but she had better things to do than to gab on the phone with him. When he answered, she told him she didn't know anything about White's and that he had the wrong number.

"You didn't do any backhauls for them?" She had to think, and told him her dad might have but he wasn't a driver anymore. "Do you think I can talk to him? Can you have him call me?"

"Might if I knew where he was. He left me high and dry about a year and a half ago. Left me with a lot of.... Like you care. I don't know where he is. And to be honest, I don't really care either." The man told her he was sorry. "Yeah, so am I. But I do have his log books. I can see what he might have done. And before you go looking into me and my truck, I had nothing to do with the missing shipments. I've been cleared."

"Missing shipments? Can you give me something on that? The company that I'm looking into, White's as I mentioned, they're missing some inventory." Hudson told him again that she'd been cleared of that mess. "I understand. But if you could help me out, I'd really appreciate it."

"I don't have any time at the moment. I'm driving now." She made the turn into the lot where she was going to see if she could rest for the night. "Look, it's past my eight and I'm dead on my ass here. Let me call you after I get some rest and grub."

"Of course. My name is Liam Harrison and the number that you called, you can call me at any time if you can." Who named their kids Liam any more, she wondered? Probably rich fucks like the company she used to work for. "Your name would be?"

"I just go by Hudson, but my first name is Emma. My dad's name is Burt Hudson. I'm sure if you do an Internet search, you can find out basically as much as I know about the missing inventory." He said he was doing that now. Of course he was, she thought. "Anyway, I'm out for the next ten or so. I'm not going to be social, so you'll have to wait. If you still need the crap I have, I'll call you in the morning."

"Thank you. You've been very helpful." She hadn't been and they both knew it. "Ms. Hudson, if you don't mind me asking, are you sure it's safe for you to be a driver?"

"It's better than my first job. Hooking paid better, but the perks weren't as good." She hung up to him sputtering on the other end. Smiling, she turned off what she could and closed her eyes for a moment.

She was exhausted. Beyond that really. She thought that she could gladly go back to bed and sleep for a month. Hudson moved to the bedroom behind her seat and looked around. It was very little compared to what she'd had over a year ago.

Her dad had left her in a bad way. The two of them had been tandem drivers since she'd convinced him to come along with her. Her mom had just left him for another life, whatever that meant, and he'd been lonely he told her. After a year on the road, just keeping her sane, Dad decided to get his CDL.

It had been fun for a while. He started talking about getting his own rig and they could double their money. She'd just paid off her own rig and house, but he'd insisted that she help him. He was her dad, he told her; his reasoning for anything that he wanted her to get for him, she realized later.

But she'd told him that things, while good, would be tight for her for a little while. Hudson explained to him, several times, that she'd been saving to get her money in order, her home paid off, and some new furniture if she could. Even though her house was paid for, he didn't need to know that.

Then about a month after she'd refused him, for the hundredth time it seemed like, he pulled up in front of her house with not only a new rig, but one that was fitted with every new gadget known to the trucking world. He even had a thirty-six-inch high definition television, big for trucks.

It wasn't until he took off that she'd found out that being her dad had been very profitable for him. When he'd disappeared, she found out that not only had he forged her name on his bank loan for his fancy new truck, but he'd also used her house as collateral. He'd even used her car, as well as her own rig, to get a few other things that she'd had no knowledge of. By the time it was done, Hudson had lost everything, including her reputation for being someone that could be trusted to get a job done.

It had taken her until just recently to get things back together. Her home was gone, and more than likely she'd never be able to have one again because of this. No car to get around, but a small bike that she'd gotten from a secondhand place. Hudson now lived in her truck for the most part, hotels when that was too much, and hadn't eaten a home cooked meal in almost eighteen months. Life, as far as she was concerned, fucking sucked.

After getting into some jeans and a sweatshirt, she made her way into the diner. Hudson didn't mind eating out, but it got old very fast when that was all your options would allow you to do. She did have boxes of cereal in her bed area, the small fridge there running off the battery, but that too was getting old.

"Whatch you wanting, darlin'?" Hudson asked for a burger and fries. "Anything to drink? Got some fresh coffee if you need it."

"Just some water please. No lemon." The waitress nodded and walked away. Hudson pulled out her dad's log books, the ones that were true, not the ones he'd forged, and started looking for anything to do with White's.

The burger was delicious, the fries a little on the soggy side, but she was too hungry to care much. The cherry pie was gross, and after only eating two bites of it, she decided that she'd rather have a week old donut than eat the rest of it. Sliding it away, she read more in the logs and made notes on all the times her dad had come out of White's with inventory.

An hour later she made her way back out to her rig to sleep, getting permission from the diner owners to sleep it off on the back of the lot having made her night. Checking her load and the tags that had been put on it when she left the lot, making sure that it matched what she had on her paperwork, Hudson climbed into her bed and closed her eyes.

Her dad had been stealing from that company. She had no idea how she knew that, but she did. And she was pretty sure that she knew who might be helping him. It was the same story that had come out twice before when he'd been investigated.

Burt would go into a company and shimmy up with one of the people working there. Tell them how millions could be made off a few dropped loads, and work the system until it ran dry or someone was beginning to ask questions. He had five businesses, six if you counted White's, that he was draining. Hudson wondered if there might be more.

Picking up her phone, she called the guy, Harrison. He answered with his last name, and she started firing questions at him. It wasn't until he asked her to slow down that she realized it was well after midnight.

"I'm sorry. I didn't think. I rarely do any more, but I'm sorry about calling so late." He told her it was okay. "No it's not. Fuck, just say, 'You dumb bitch, don't you fucking know what time it is?' Stop being so nice before someone takes you to the cleaner."

"Is that what he did to you?" Hudson felt the pain of her dad's betrayal in her heart when Liam's question came across the line. "I read about it. I had one of my sisters-in-law dig a little deeper too. He really screwed you over."

"He did, but that's not really your concern, is it? Look, I'm sorry I called so late, but here's the deal. He did haul for White's. A total of nineteen times from January of the year before until about sixteen months ago, just about the time shit hit the fan." He told her that it wasn't in the paperwork from the trial. "Yeah, well they didn't have his books."

"You mean his own books, not the ones that were found in his truck." She told him most drivers had two logs, so it wasn't a big deal. "But I'm betting you don't, do you? I read about you as well."

"Look Mr. Harrison, what I did or don't do is none of your concern. If you want these log books, then I'll send them to you. But as far as getting up close and into my personal shit, let's just say that's never going to happen." He apologized again. "Do you have any idea how many times I've had to say that to someone and mean it only to have it blown back in my face? More than you can count. Just give me your address and I'll sent this shit to you."

He did, and didn't, thankfully, say he was sorry again. But before she could say anything more, she closed the connection. Christ, she did not need this today. Looking at her clock, Hudson realized it was her birthday.

"Happy fucking birthday." Rolling to her side in the little bed, she thought of how angry she'd been at Liam. He'd done nothing wrong to her, yet she'd been a royal fucking cunt to him. Looking at the address again for where he was, she realized that she was less than two hours from him, and his location was on her way back to her next load. Deciding that she'd been a bitch enough for one day, she checked the rig once more and then locked herself in. Tomorrow would be better, even if she had to kill someone to make it happen.

189

Before You Go...

HELP AN AUTHOR

write a review

THANK YOU!

Share your voice and help guide other readers to these wonderful books. Even if it's only a line or two your reviews help readers discover the author's books so they can continue creating stories that you'll love. Login to your favorite retailer and leave a review. Thank you.

AWARD WINNING, BESTSELLING AUTHOR

Kathi Barton, author of the bestselling series Force of Nature, lives in Nashport, Ohio with her husband, Paul. In addition to writing full time Kathi likes to spend time with her eight grandkids, three children and three children-in-laws. She writes to relax and have fun.

Her muse, a cross between Jimmy Stewart and Hugh Jackman, brings them to life for her readers in a way that has them coming back time and again for more. Her favorite genre is paranormal romance with a great deal of spice. You can visit Kathi online and drop her an email if you'd like. She loves hearing from her fans. aaronskiss@gmail.com.

Follow Kathi on her blog: http://kathisbartonauthor.blogspot.com/